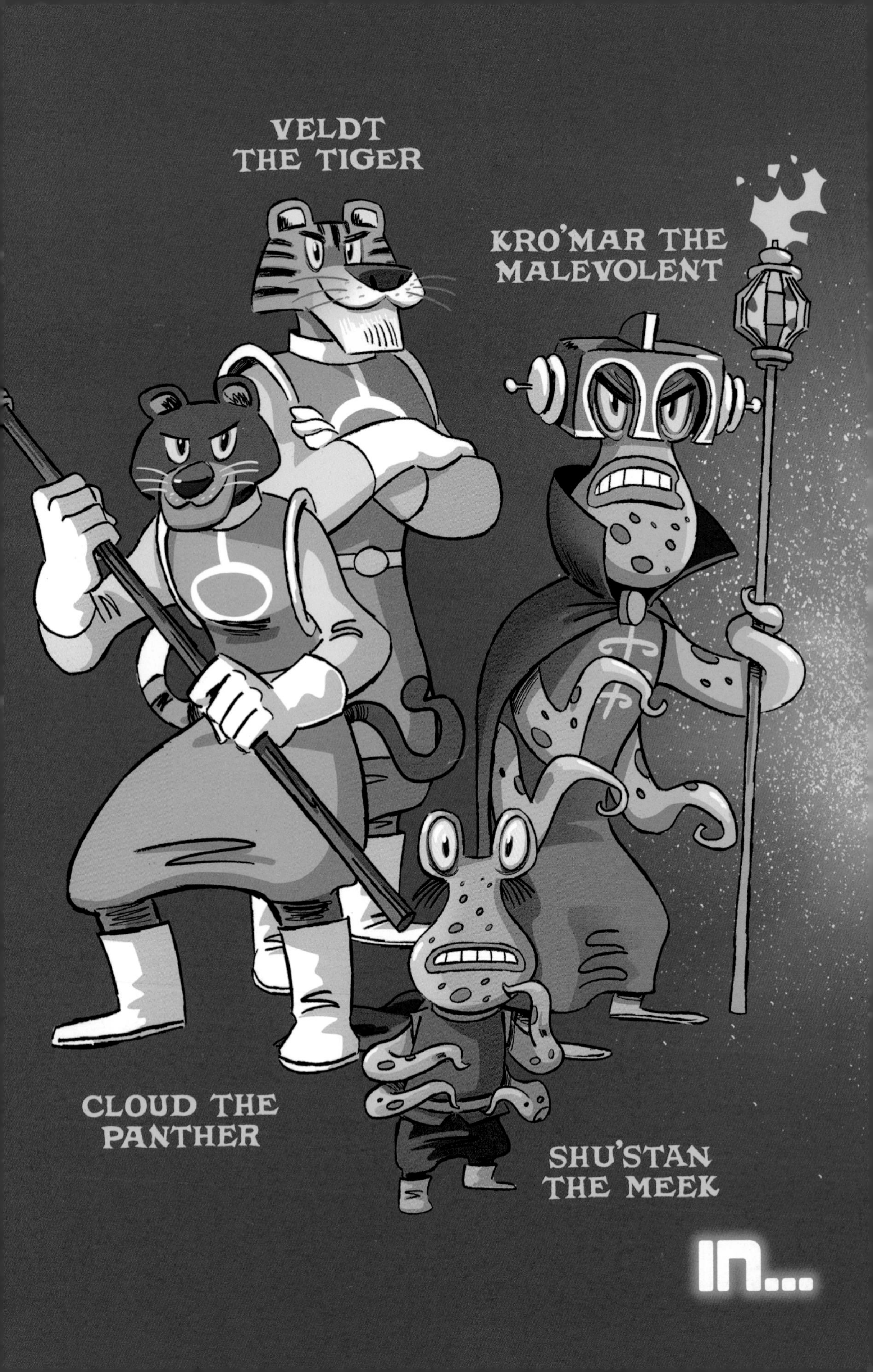
VELDT THE TIGER
KRO'MAR THE MALEVOLENT
CLOUD THE PANTHER
SHU'STAN THE MEEK
IN...

Far Out Fables is published by
Stone Arch Books
A Capstone Imprint
1710 Roe Crest Drive
North Mankato, Minnesota 56003
www.mycapstone.com

Cataloging-in-Publication Data is
available at the Library of Congress
website.
ISBN 978-1-4965-5422-2 (hardcover)
ISBN 978-1-4965-5426-0 (paperback)
ISBN 978-1-4965-5430-7 (eBook PDF)

Summary: Aliens are invading! Mighty
Thunder the Lion is leading the fight to
free Earth from the aliens, the Zurg.
Daisy the Mouse rushes to join the
cause, only to be laughed out by the
lion and his troops. But when Thunder
is taken prisoner, it's up to Daisy to
rescue him. Can Daisy and Thunder
team up to beat the extraterrestrial
threat once and for all?

Designed by Hilary Wacholz
Edited by Abby Huff
Lettered by Jaymes Reed

Printed in the USA.
102018   001127

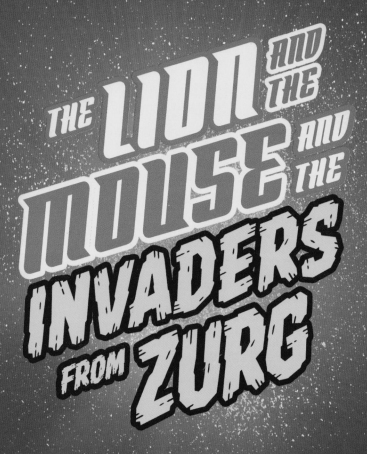

FAR OUT FABLES

THE LION AND THE MOUSE AND THE INVADERS FROM ZURG

A GRAPHIC NOVEL

BY BENJAMIN HARPER

ILLUSTRATED BY PEDRO RODRIGUEZ

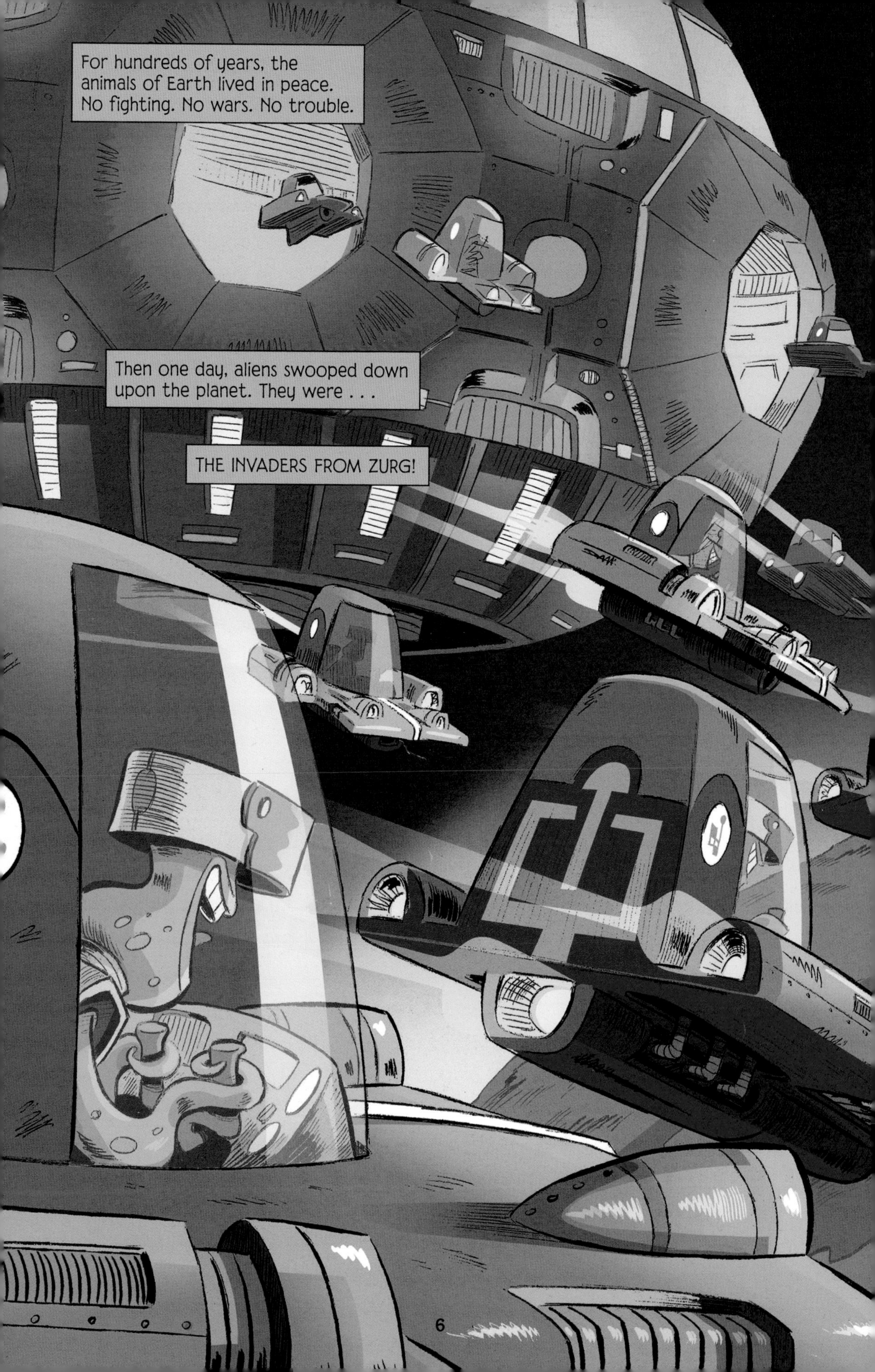
For hundreds of years, the animals of Earth lived in peace. No fighting. No wars. No trouble.
Then one day, aliens swooped down upon the planet. They were . . .
THE INVADERS FROM ZURG!

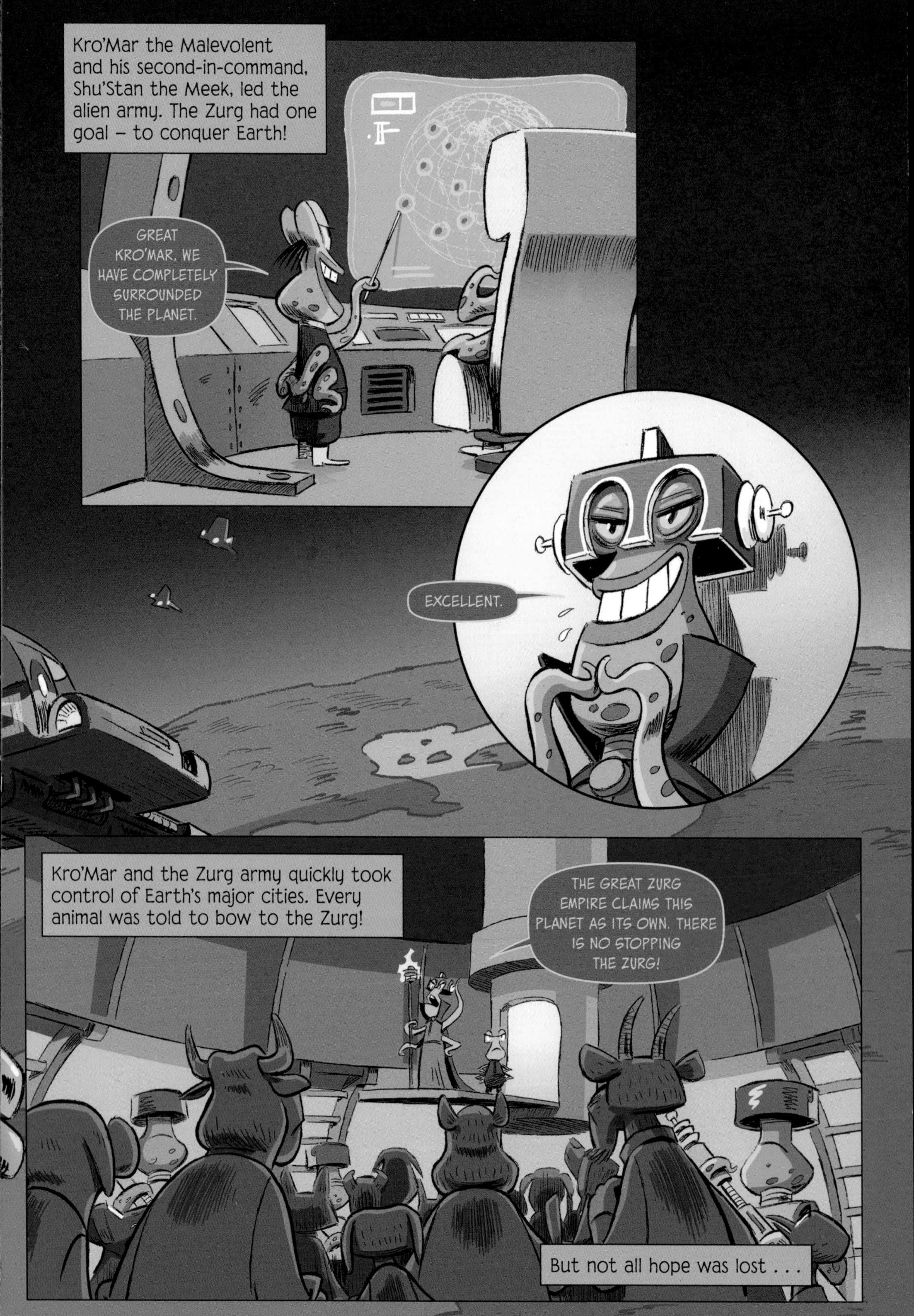
Kro'Mar the Malevolent and his second-in-command, Shu'Stan the Meek, led the alien army. The Zurg had one goal – to conquer Earth!
GREAT KRO'MAR, WE HAVE COMPLETELY SURROUNDED THE PLANET.
EXCELLENT.
Kro'Mar and the Zurg army quickly took control of Earth's major cities. Every animal was told to bow to the Zurg!
THE GREAT ZURG EMPIRE CLAIMS THIS PLANET AS ITS OWN. THERE IS NO STOPPING THE ZURG!
But not all hope was lost . . .

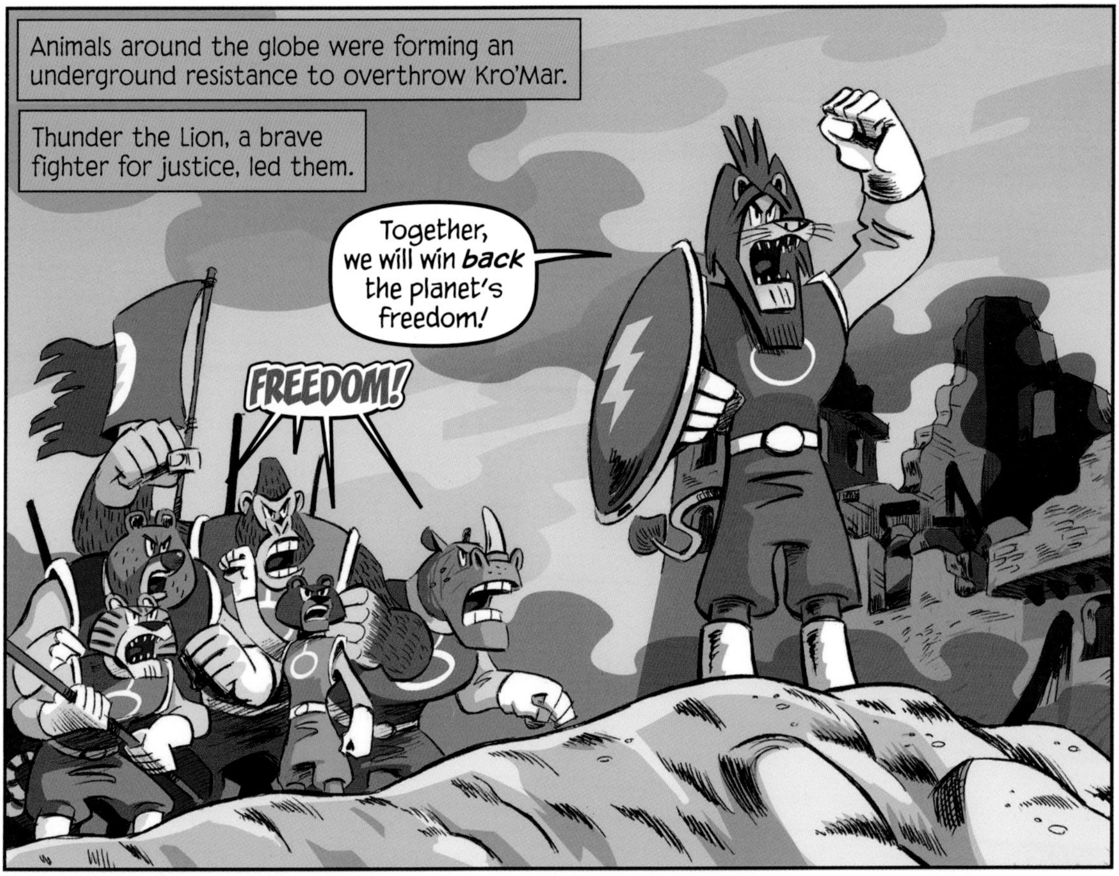
Animals around the globe were forming an underground resistance to overthrow Kro'Mar.
Thunder the Lion, a brave fighter for justice, led them.
Together, we will win *back* the planet's freedom!
FREEDOM!

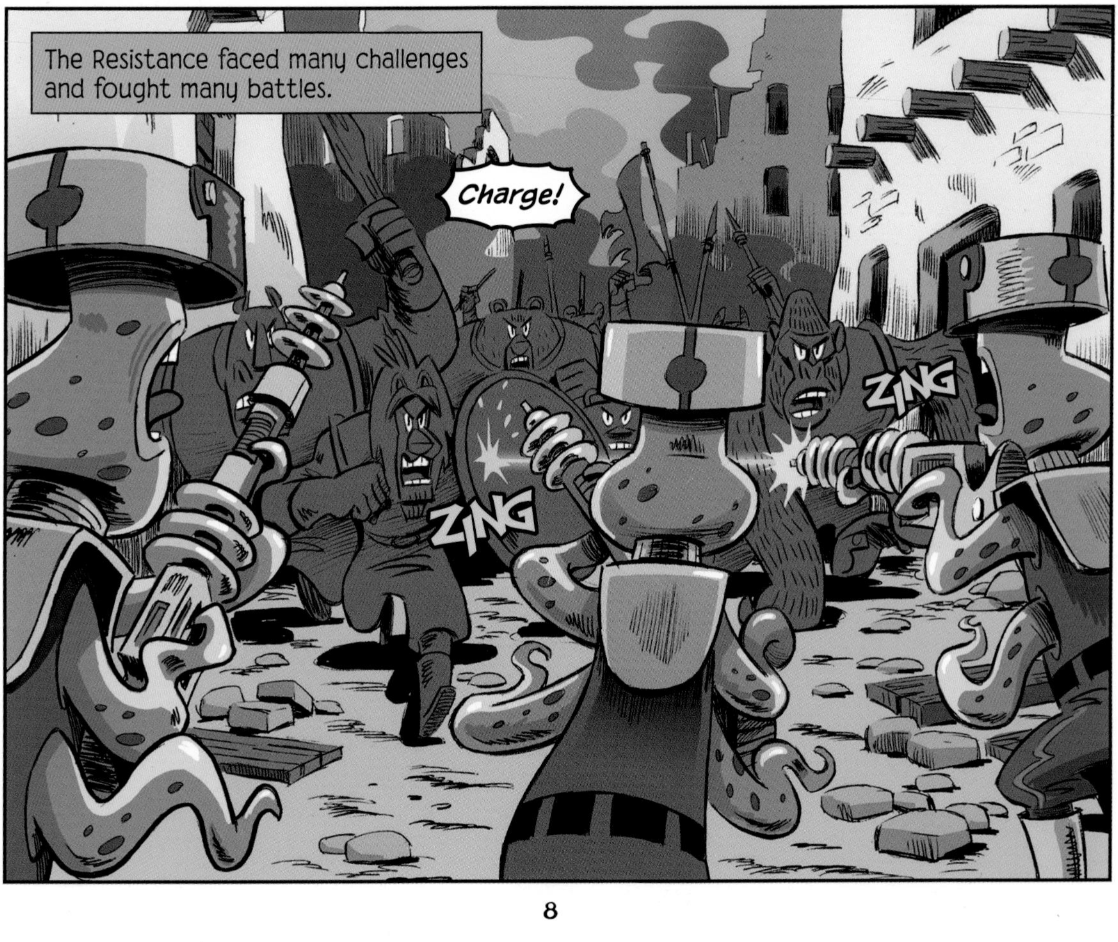
The Resistance faced many challenges and fought many battles.
Charge!
ZING
ZING

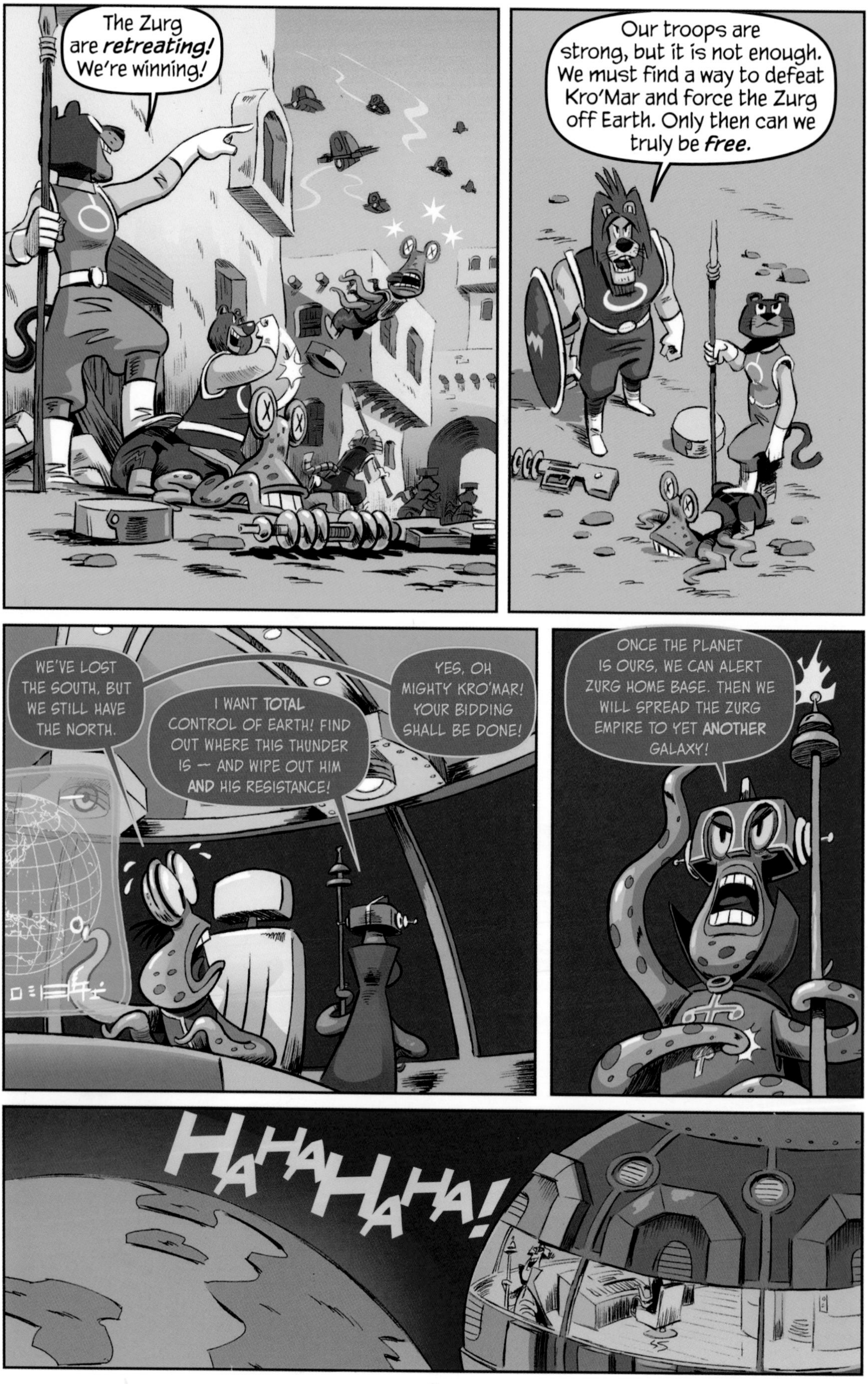
The Zurg are *retreating!* We're winning!
Our troops are strong, but it is not enough. We must find a way to defeat Kro'Mar and force the Zurg off Earth. Only then can we truly be *free.*
WE'VE LOST THE SOUTH, BUT WE STILL HAVE THE NORTH.
I WANT **TOTAL** CONTROL OF EARTH! FIND OUT WHERE THIS THUNDER IS — AND WIPE OUT HIM **AND** HIS RESISTANCE!
YES, OH MIGHTY KRO'MAR! YOUR BIDDING SHALL BE DONE!
ONCE THE PLANET IS OURS, WE CAN ALERT ZURG HOME BASE. THEN WE WILL SPREAD THE ZURG EMPIRE TO YET **ANOTHER** GALAXY!
HAHAHAHAHA!

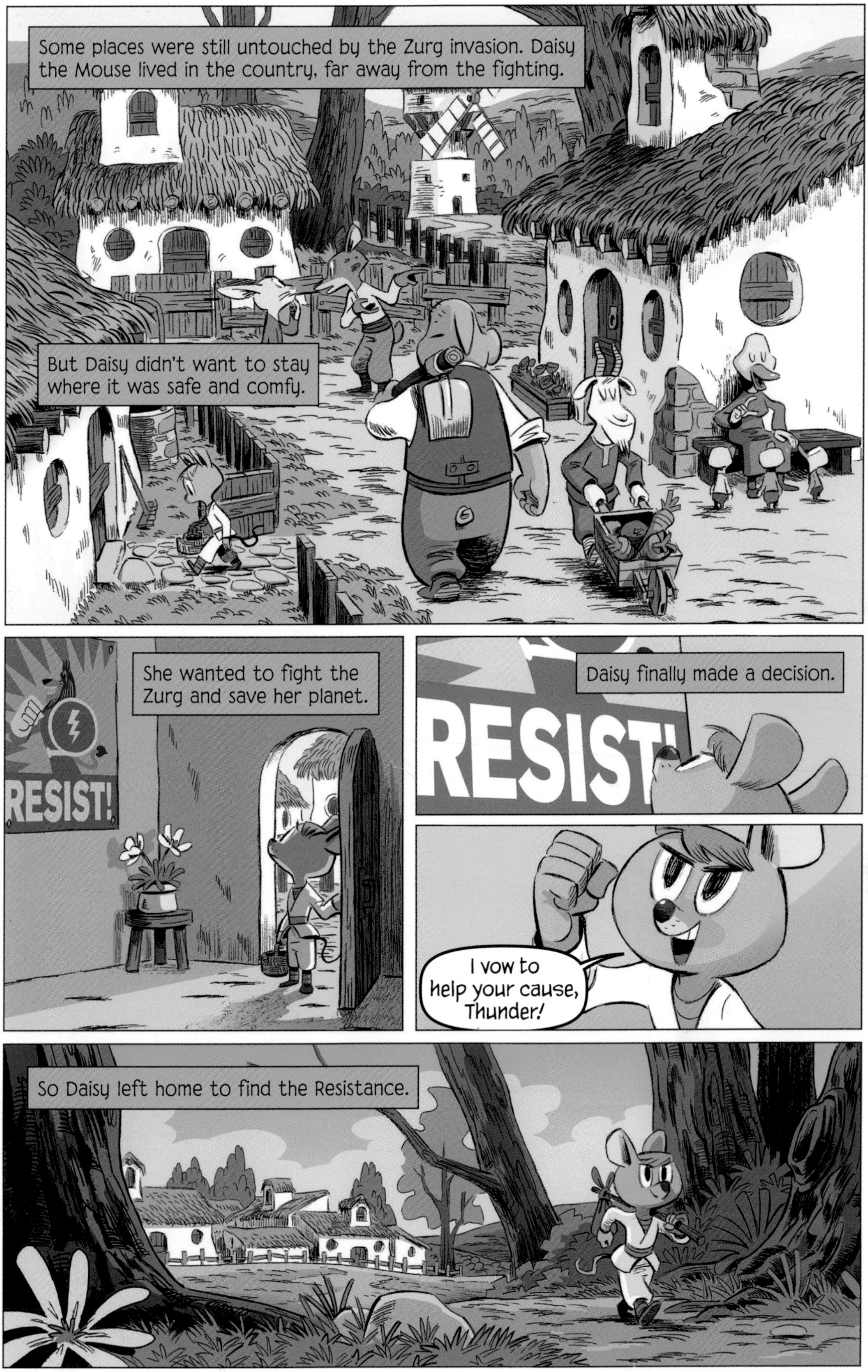
Some places were still untouched by the Zurg invasion. Daisy the Mouse lived in the country, far away from the fighting.
But Daisy didn't want to stay where it was safe and comfy.
RESIST!
She wanted to fight the Zurg and save her planet.
Daisy finally made a decision.
RESIST!
I vow to help your cause, Thunder!
So Daisy left home to find the Resistance.

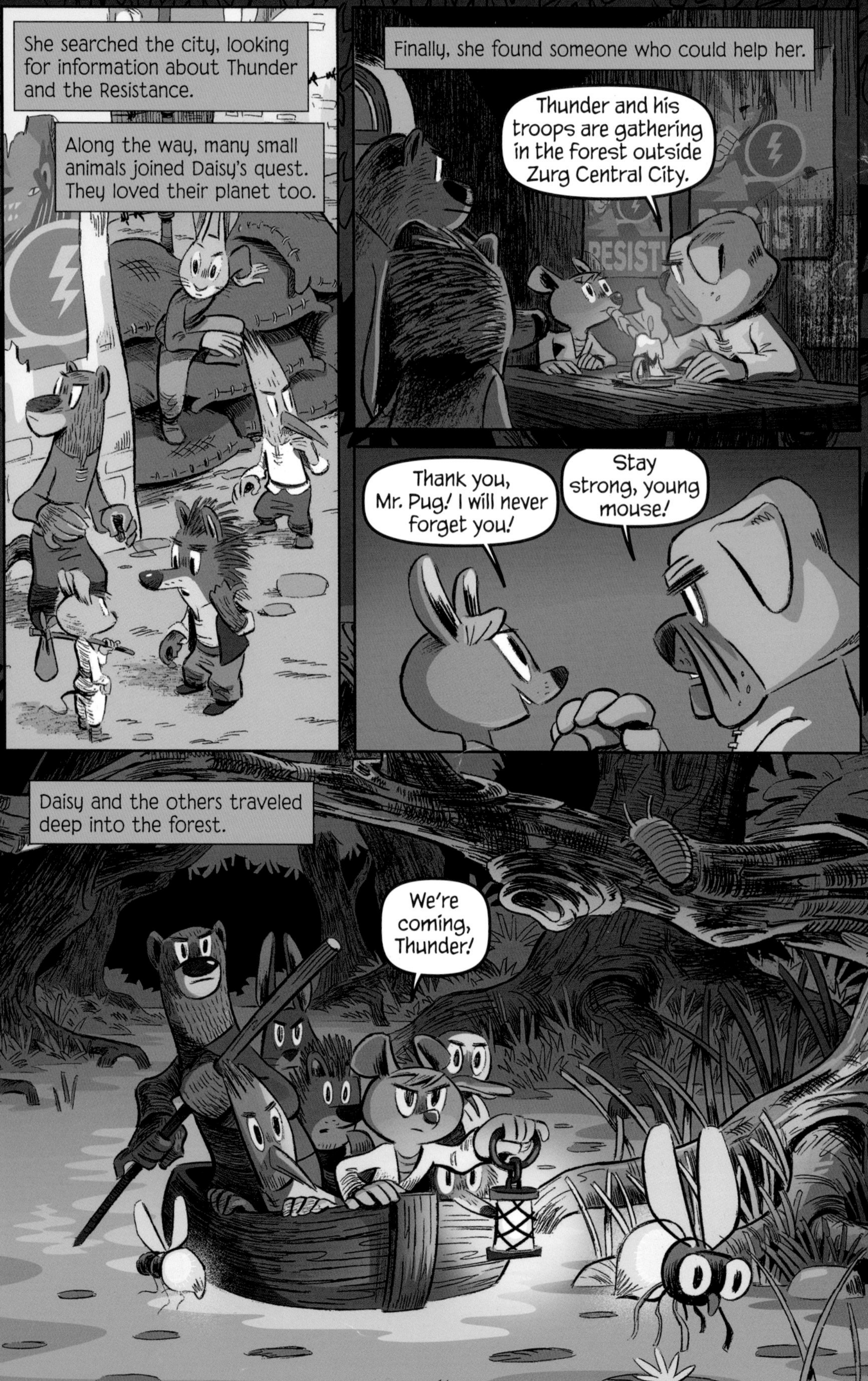
She searched the city, looking for information about Thunder and the Resistance.
Along the way, many small animals joined Daisy's quest. They loved their planet too.
Finally, she found someone who could help her.
Thunder and his troops are gathering in the forest outside Zurg Central City.
RESIST!
Thank you, Mr. Pug! I will never forget you!
Stay strong, young mouse!
Daisy and the others traveled deep into the forest.
We're coming, Thunder!

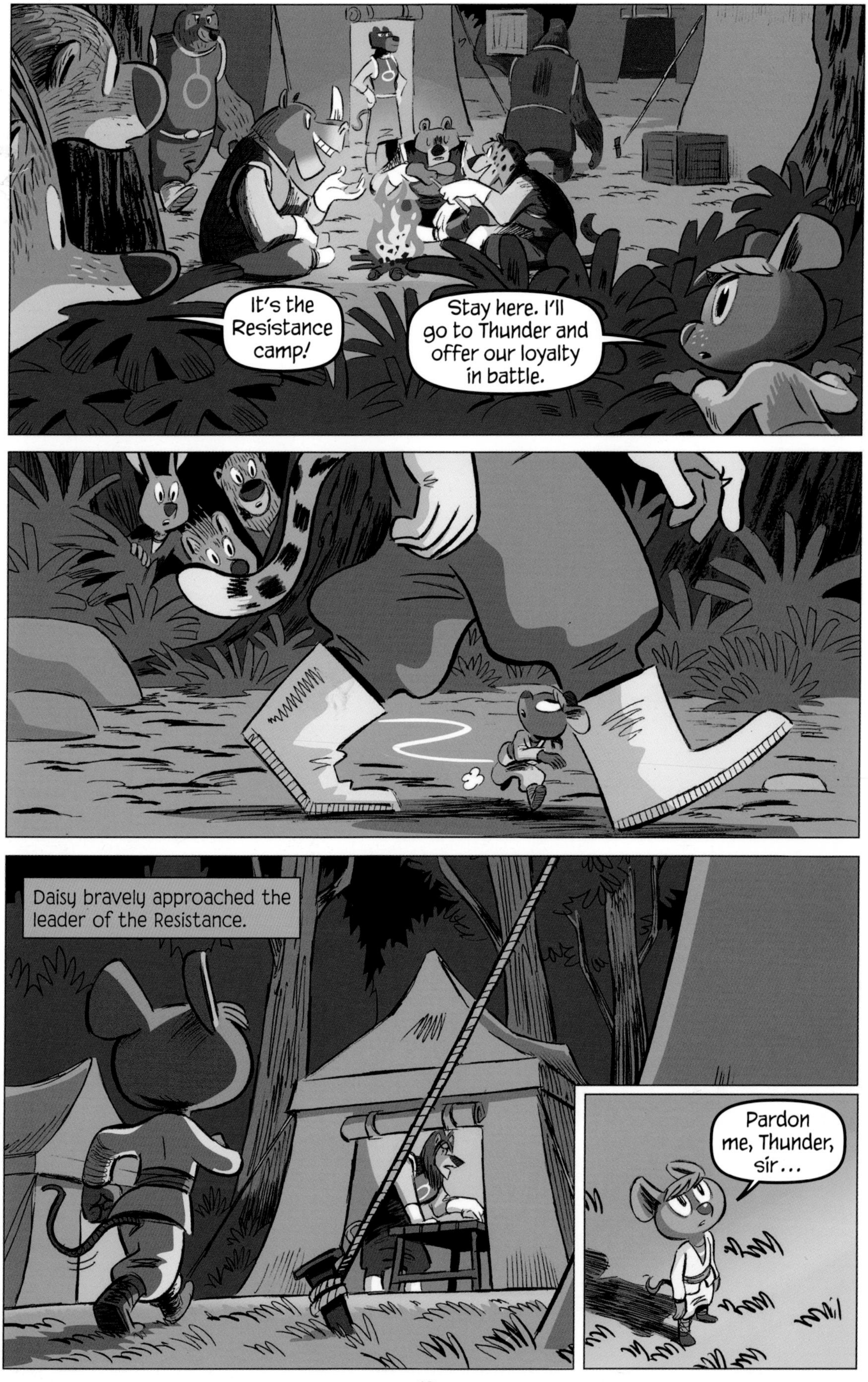
It's the Resistance camp!
Stay here. I'll go to Thunder and offer our loyalty in battle.
Daisy bravely approached the leader of the Resistance.
Pardon me, Thunder, sir...

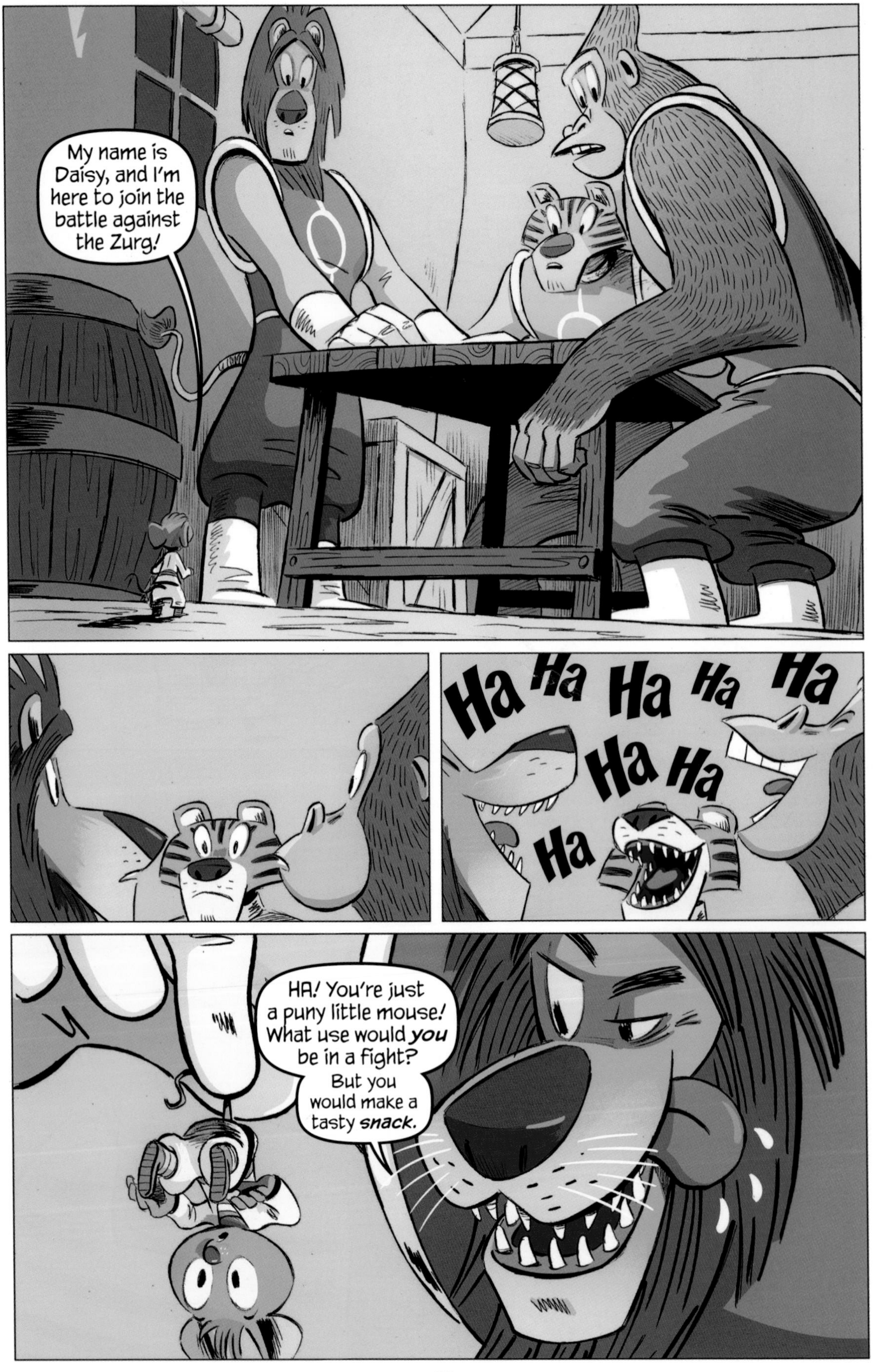
My name is Daisy, and I'm here to join the battle against the Zurg!
Ha Ha Ha Ha Ha Ha Ha Ha
HA! You're just a puny little mouse! What use would *you* be in a fight?
But you would make a tasty ***snack***.

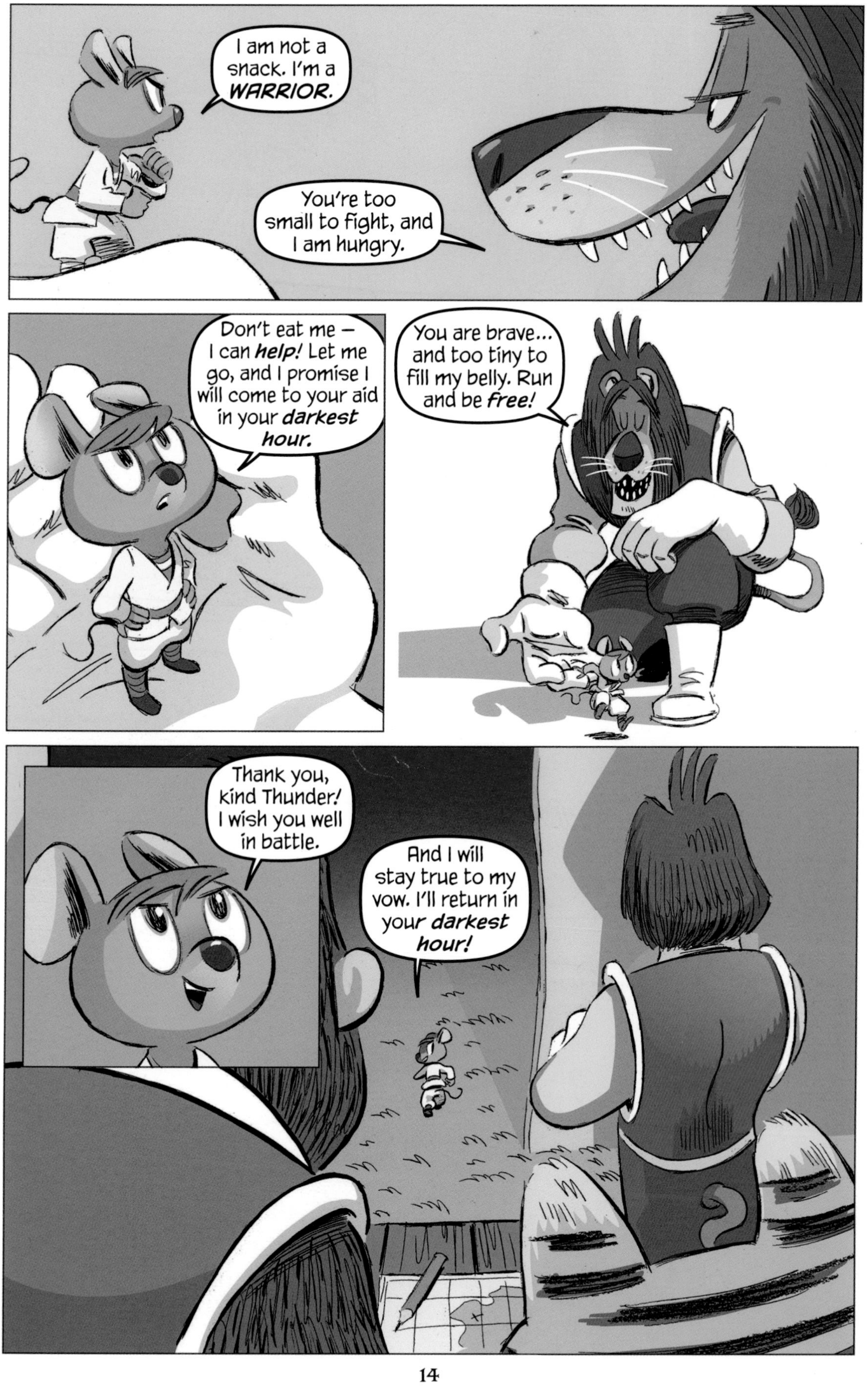
I am not a snack. I'm a ***WARRIOR.***
You're too small to fight, and I am hungry.
Don't eat me — I can ***help!*** Let me go, and I promise I will come to your aid in your ***darkest hour.***
You are brave... and too tiny to fill my belly. Run and be ***free!***
Thank you, kind Thunder! I wish you well in battle.
And I will stay true to my vow. I'll return in your ***darkest hour!***

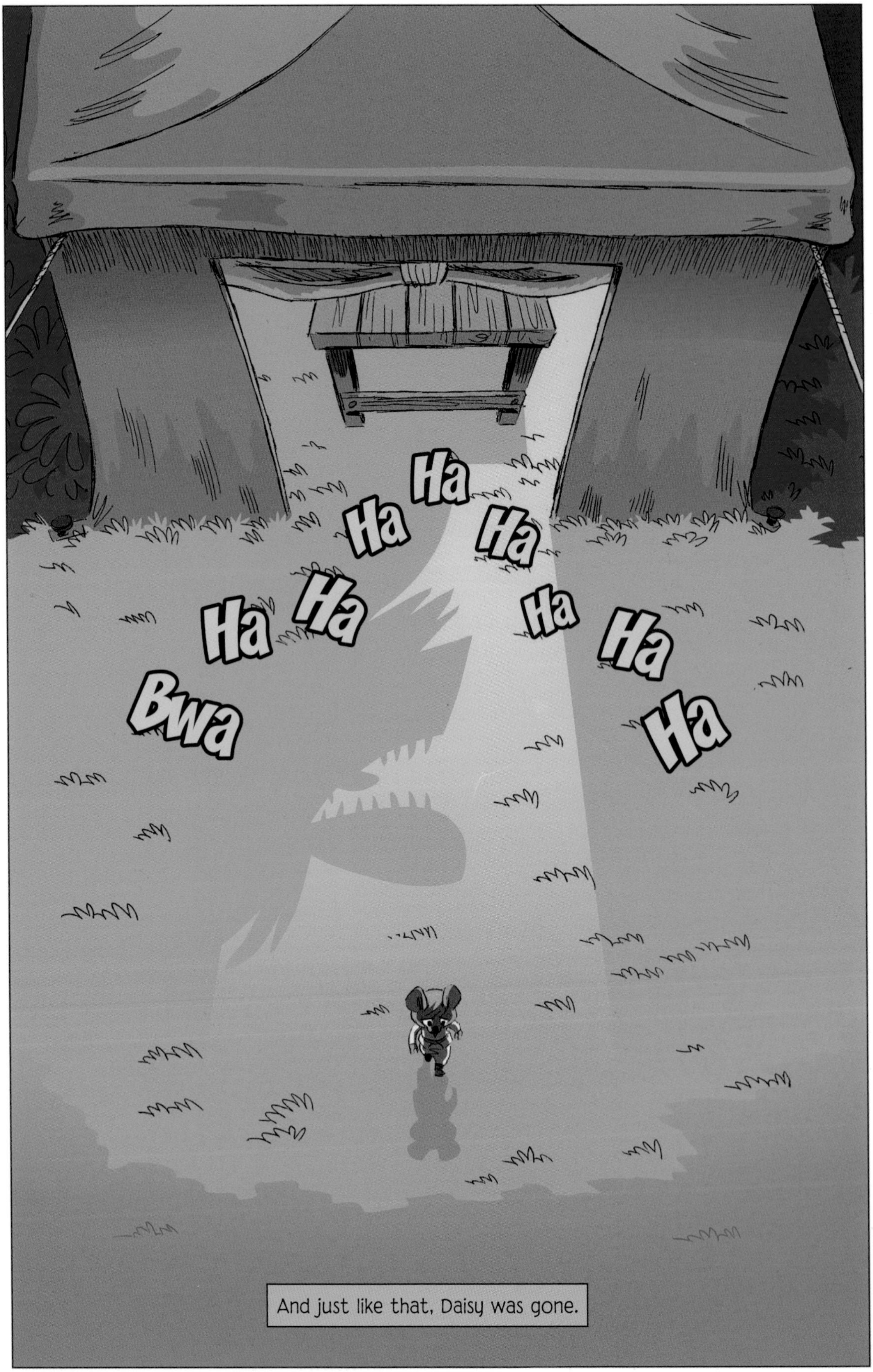
Bwa
Ha
Ha
Ha
Ha
Ha
Ha
Ha
Ha
And just like that, Daisy was gone.

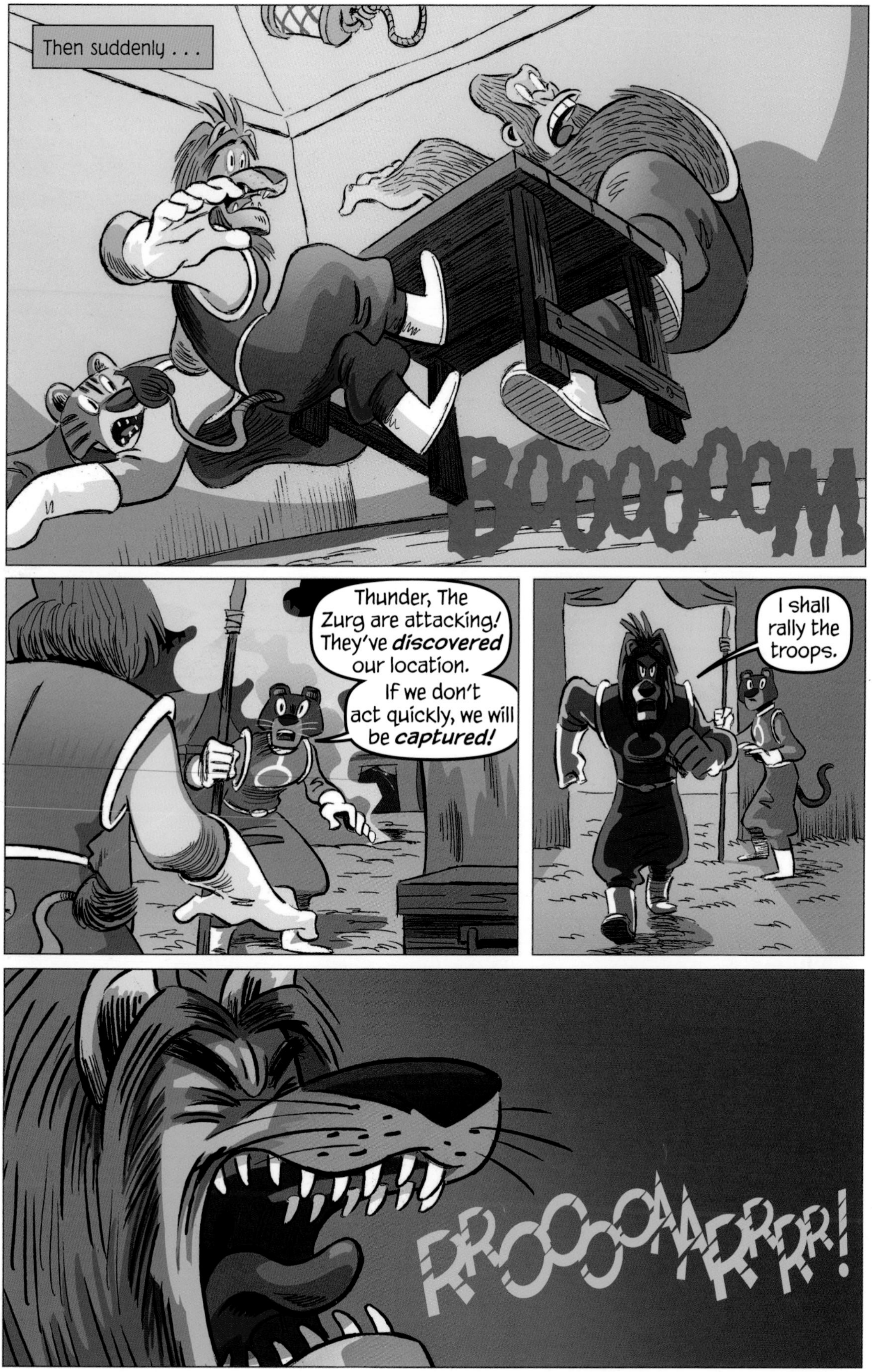
Then suddenly . . .
BOOOOOOM
Thunder, The Zurg are attacking! They've *discovered* our location.
If we don't act quickly, we will be *captured!*
I shall rally the troops.
RROOOOAARRRR!

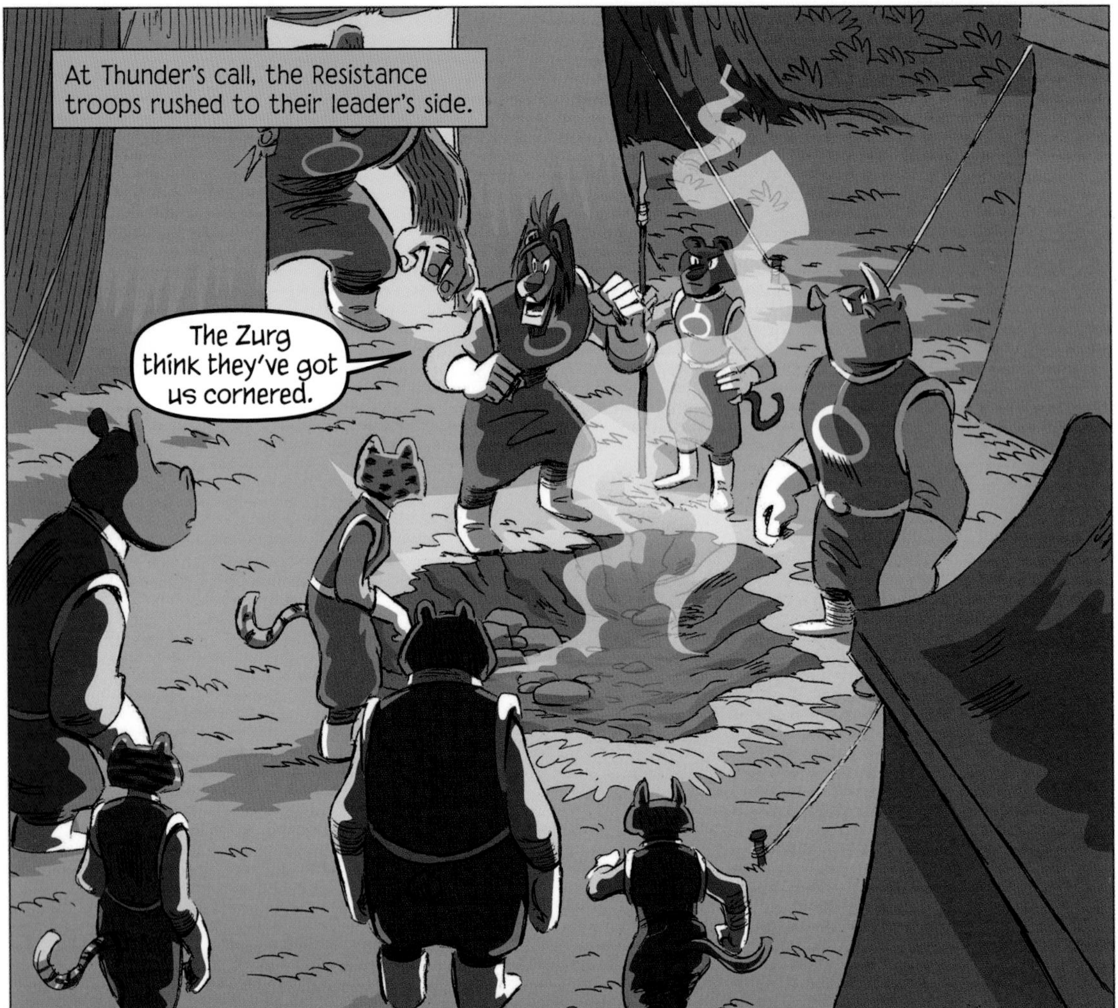
At Thunder's call, the Resistance troops rushed to their leader's side.
The Zurg think they've got us cornered.

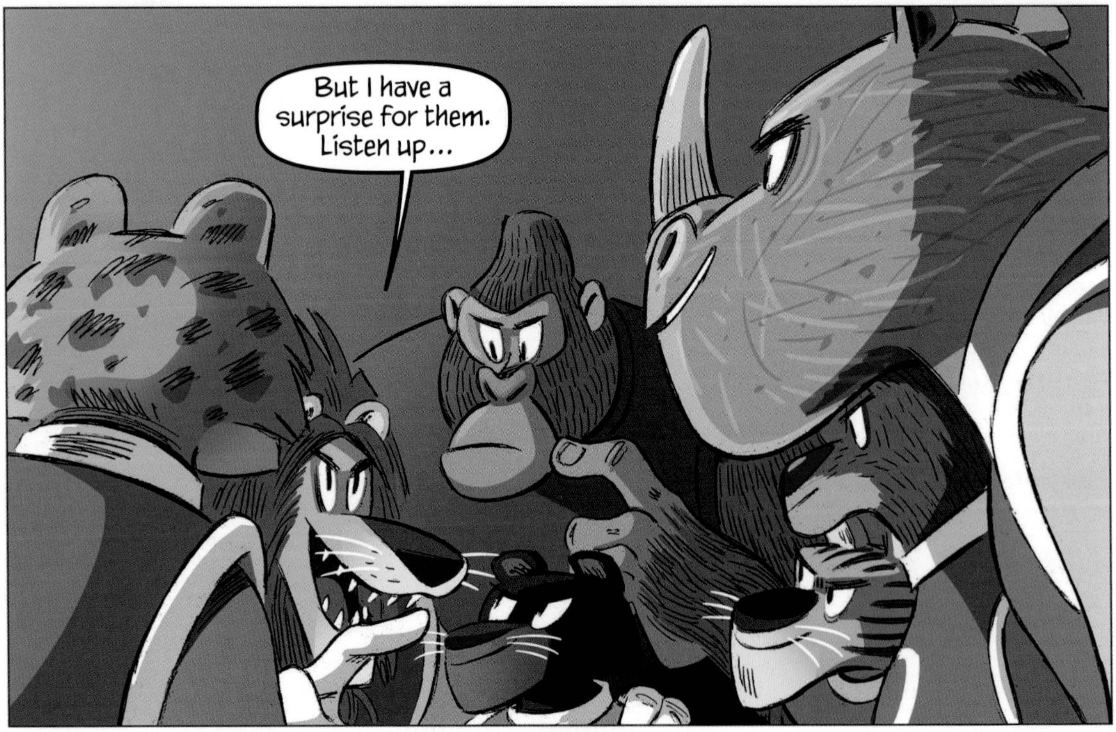
But I have a surprise for them. Listen up...

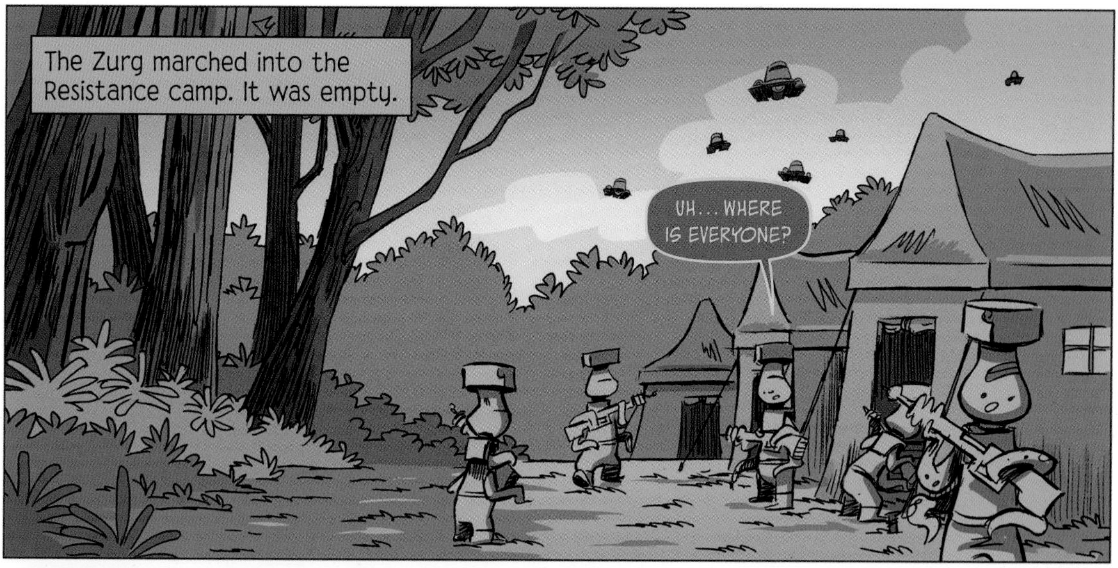
The Zurg marched into the Resistance camp. It was empty.
UH . . . WHERE IS EVERYONE?

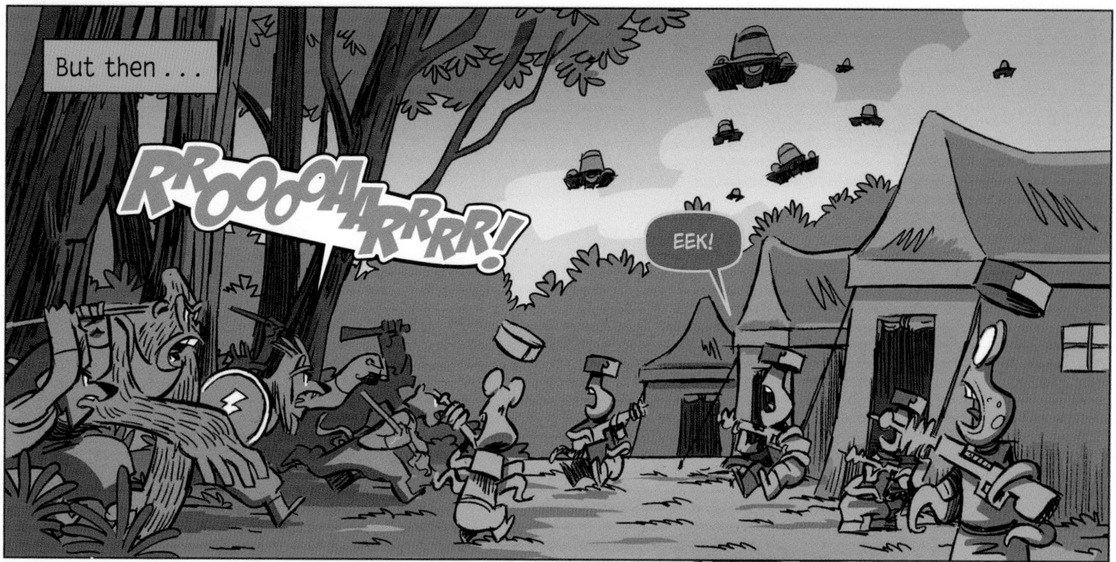
But then . . .
RROOOOOAARRRRR!
EEK!

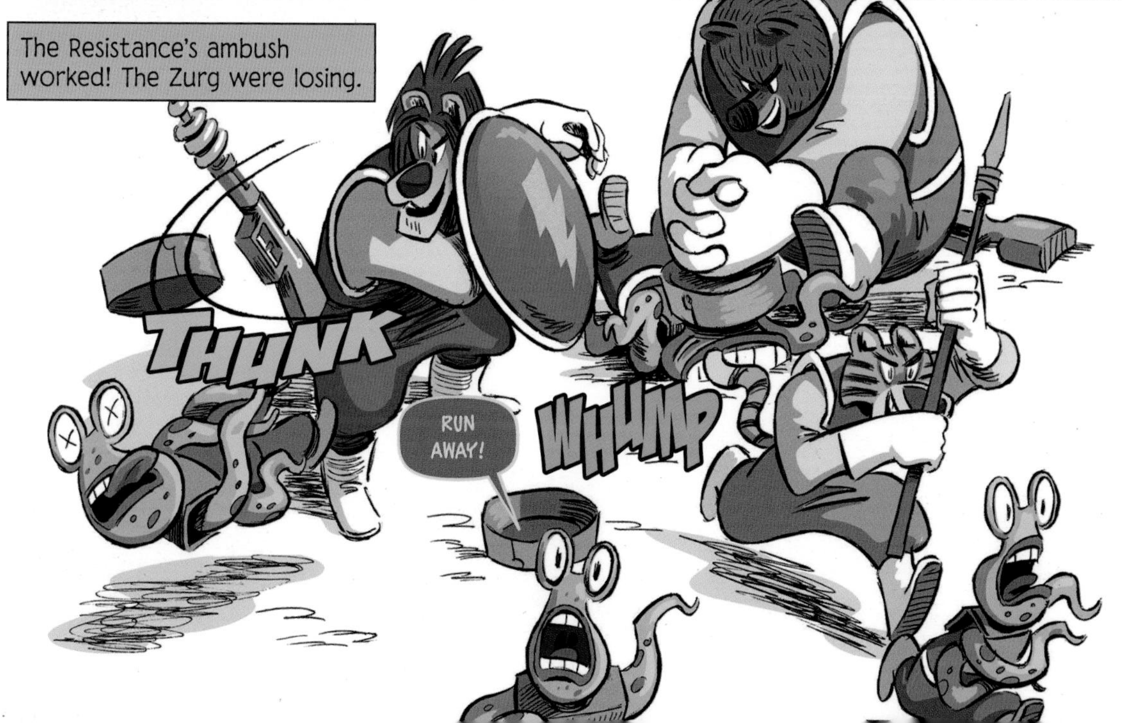
The Resistance's ambush worked! The Zurg were losing.
THUNK
RUN AWAY!
WHUMP

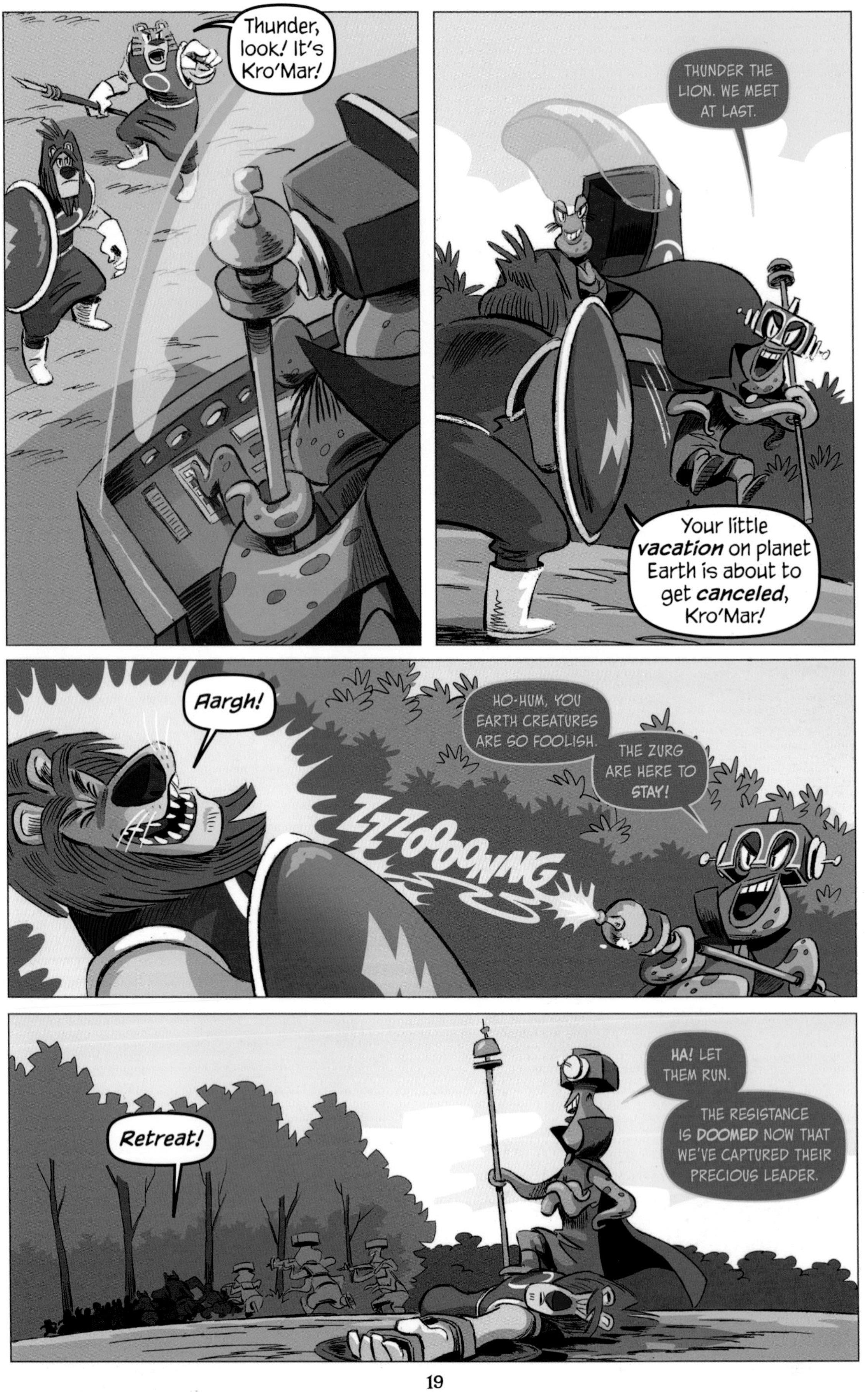

Thunder, look! It's Kro'Mar!
THUNDER THE LION. WE MEET AT LAST.
Your little *vacation* on planet Earth is about to get *canceled*, Kro'Mar!
Aargh!
HO-HUM, YOU EARTH CREATURES ARE SO FOOLISH.
THE ZURG ARE HERE TO STAY!
ZZZOOOONNG
Retreat!
HA! LET THEM RUN.
THE RESISTANCE IS DOOMED NOW THAT WE'VE CAPTURED THEIR PRECIOUS LEADER.

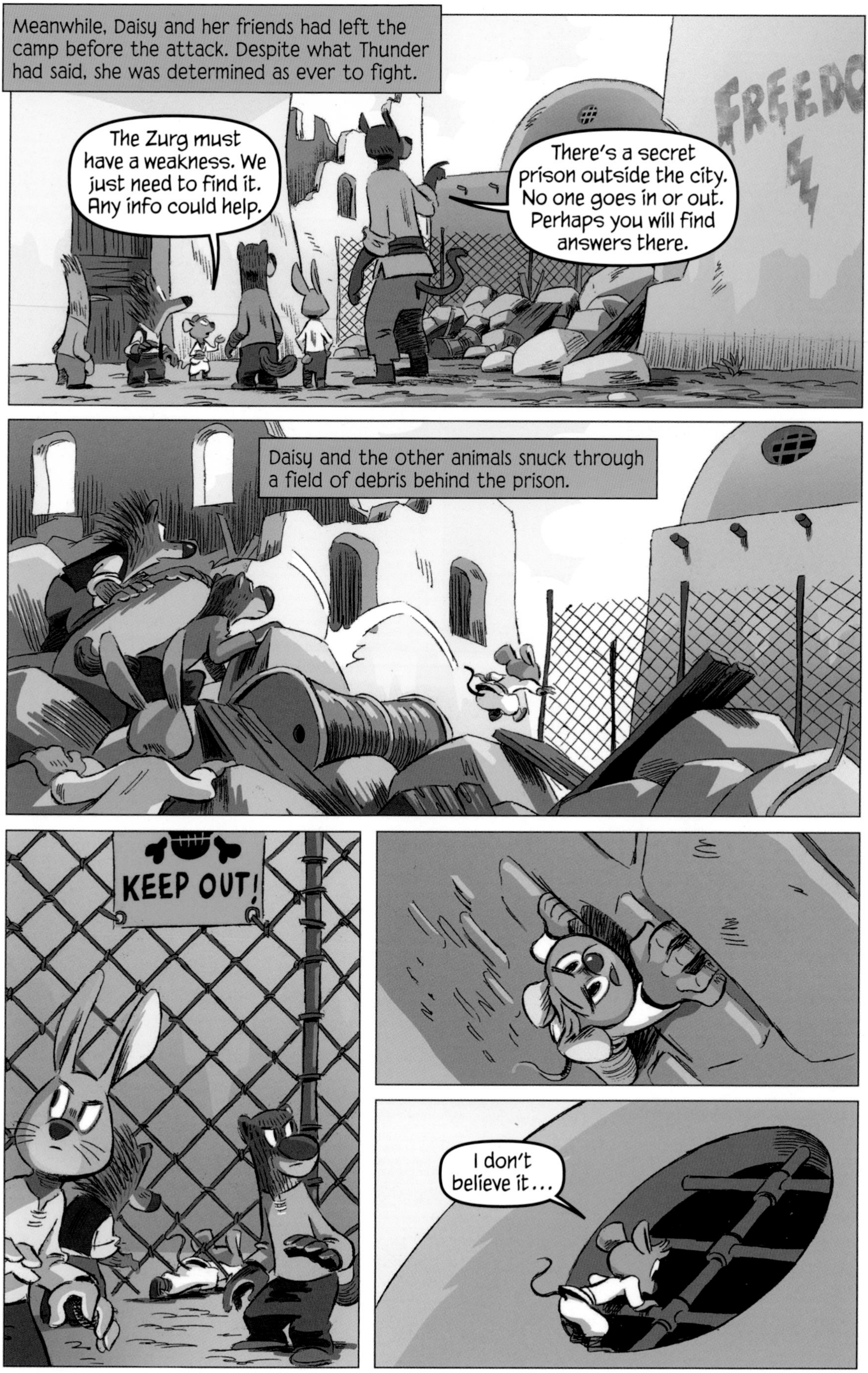
Meanwhile, Daisy and her friends had left the camp before the attack. Despite what Thunder had said, she was determined as ever to fight.
The Zurg must have a weakness. We just need to find it. Any info could help.
There's a secret prison outside the city. No one goes in or out. Perhaps you will find answers there.
Daisy and the other animals snuck through a field of debris behind the prison.
KEEP OUT!
I don't believe it...

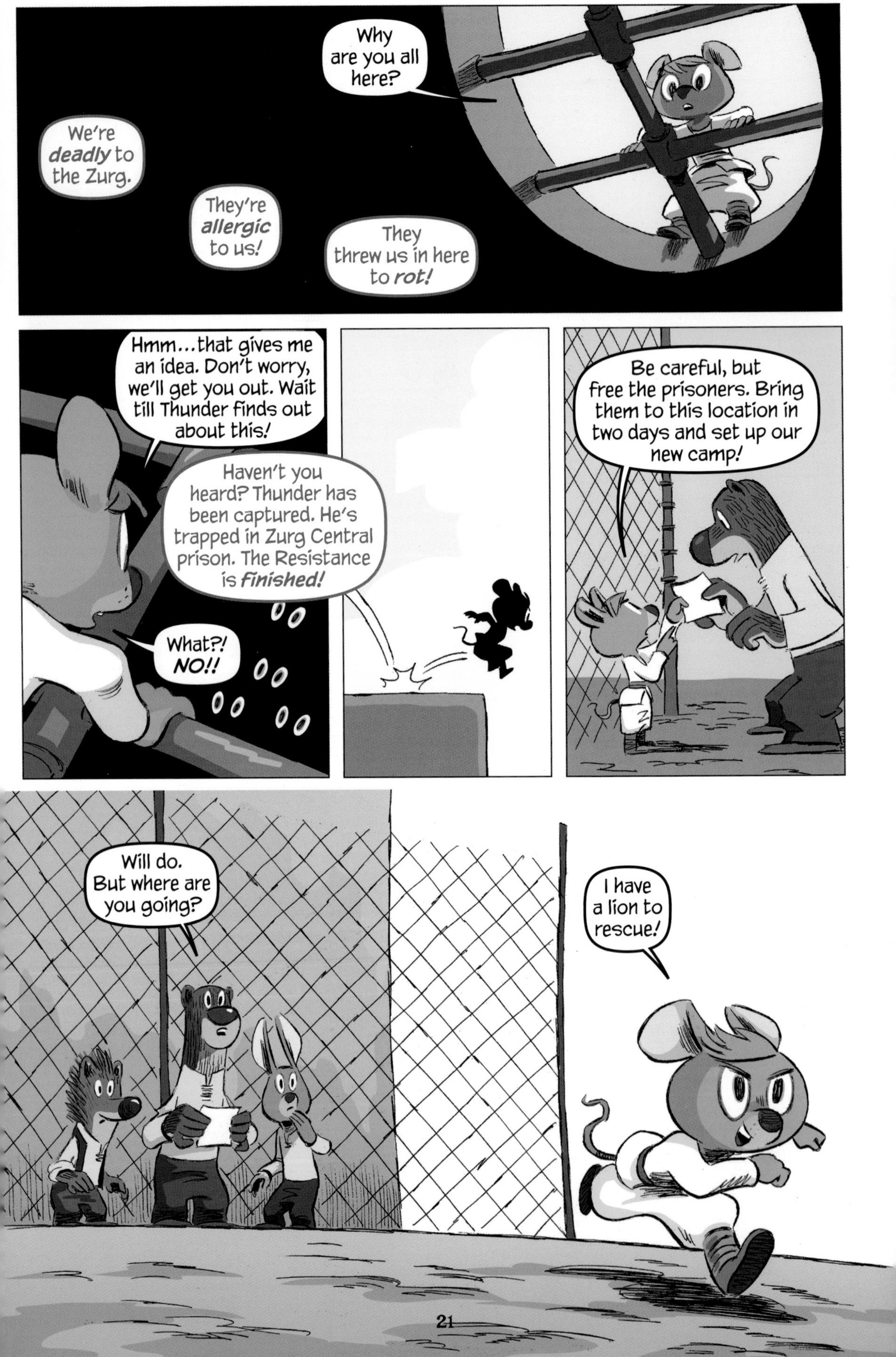
Why are you all here?
We're *deadly* to the Zurg.
They're *allergic* to us!
They threw us in here to *rot!*
Hmm...that gives me an idea. Don't worry, we'll get you out. Wait till Thunder finds out about this!
Haven't you heard? Thunder has been captured. He's trapped in Zurg Central prison. The Resistance is *Finished!*
What?! *NO!!*
Be careful, but free the prisoners. Bring them to this location in two days and set up our new camp!
Will do. But where are you going?
I have a lion to rescue!

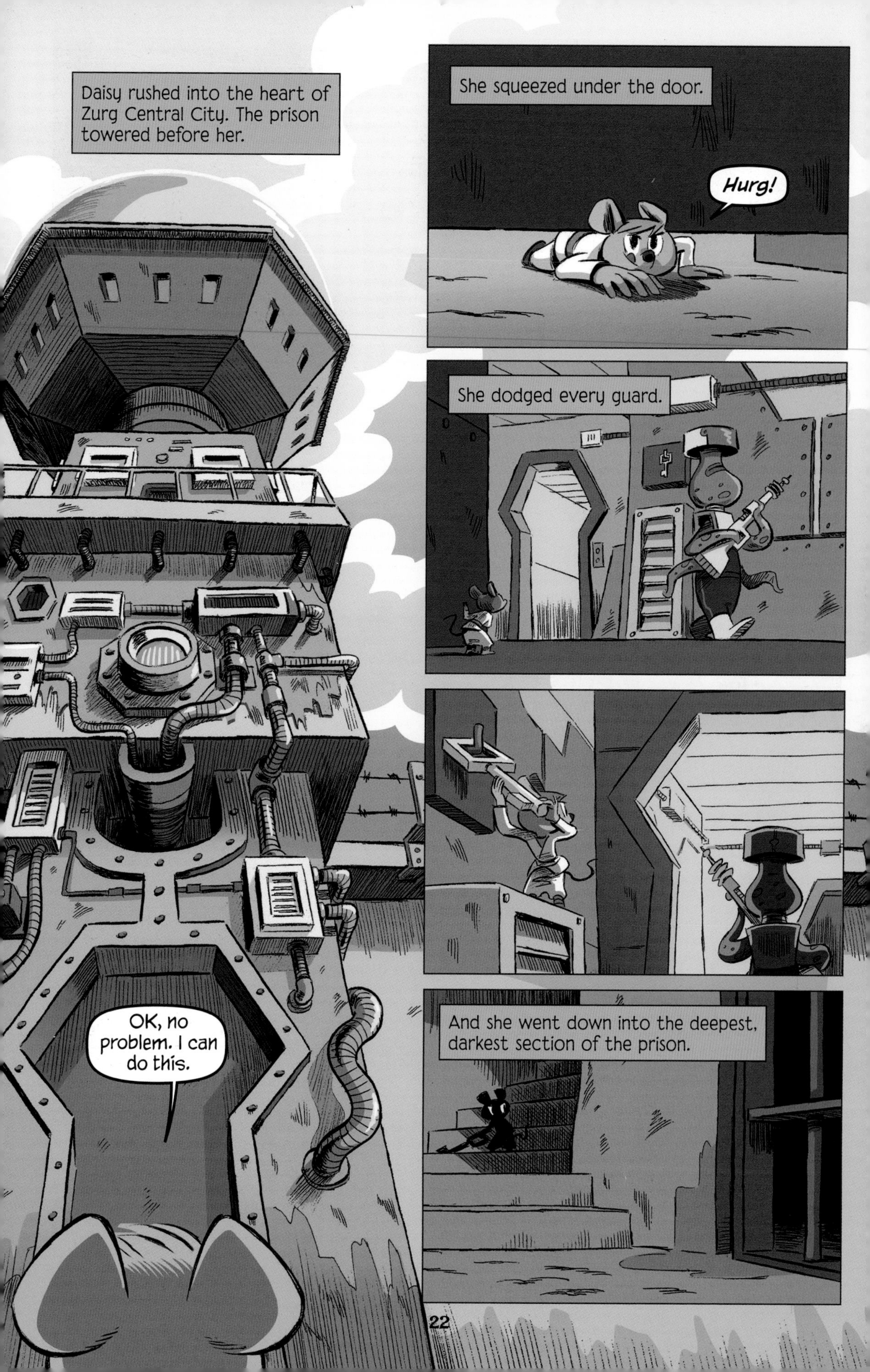
Daisy rushed into the heart of Zurg Central City. The prison towered before her.
OK, no problem. I can do this.
She squeezed under the door.
Hurg!
She dodged every guard.
And she went down into the deepest, darkest section of the prison.

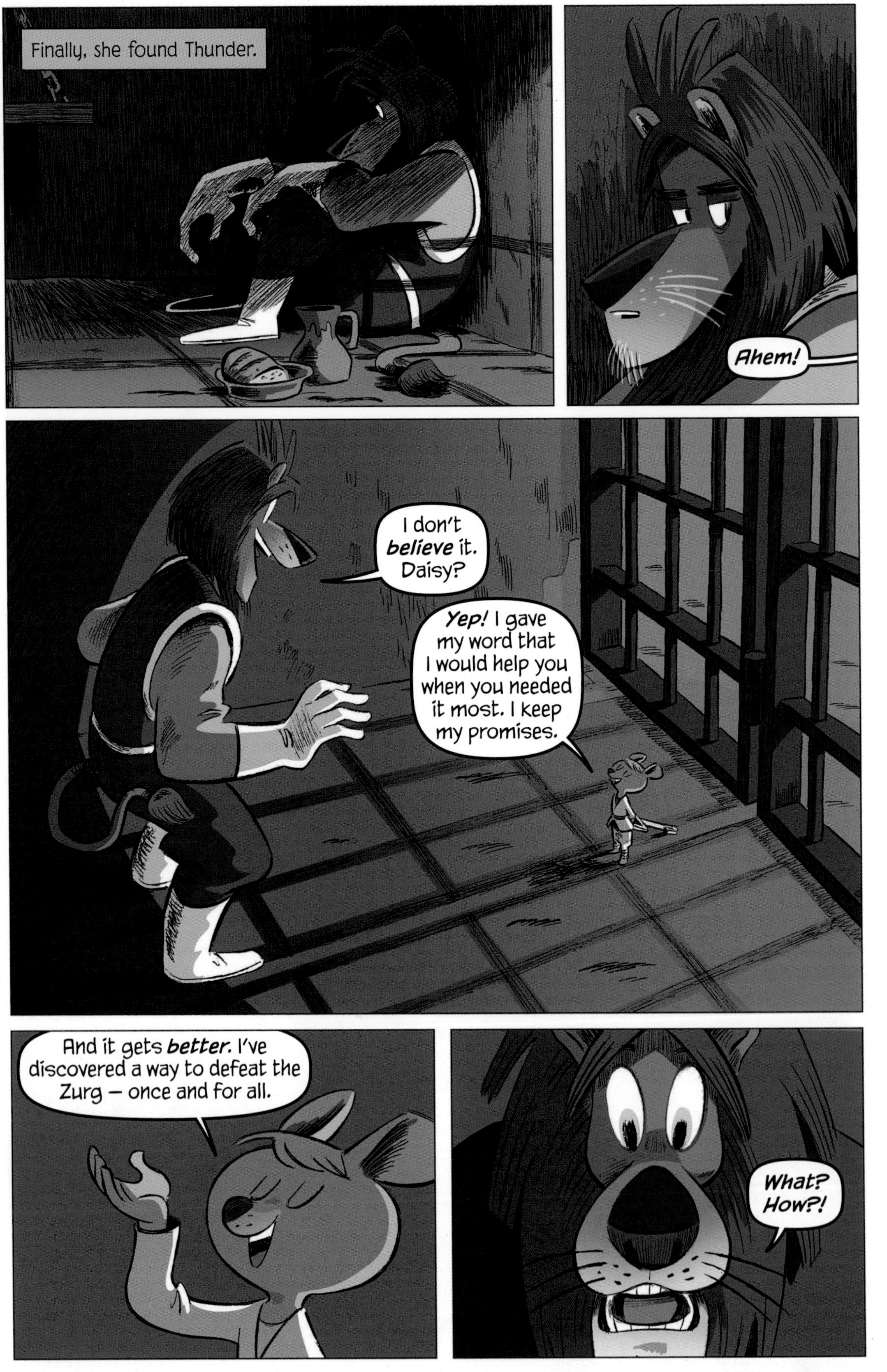
Finally, she found Thunder.
Ahem!
I don't *believe* it. Daisy?
Yep! I gave my word that I would help you when you needed it most. I keep my promises.
And it gets *better.* I've discovered a way to defeat the Zurg — once and for all.
What? How?!

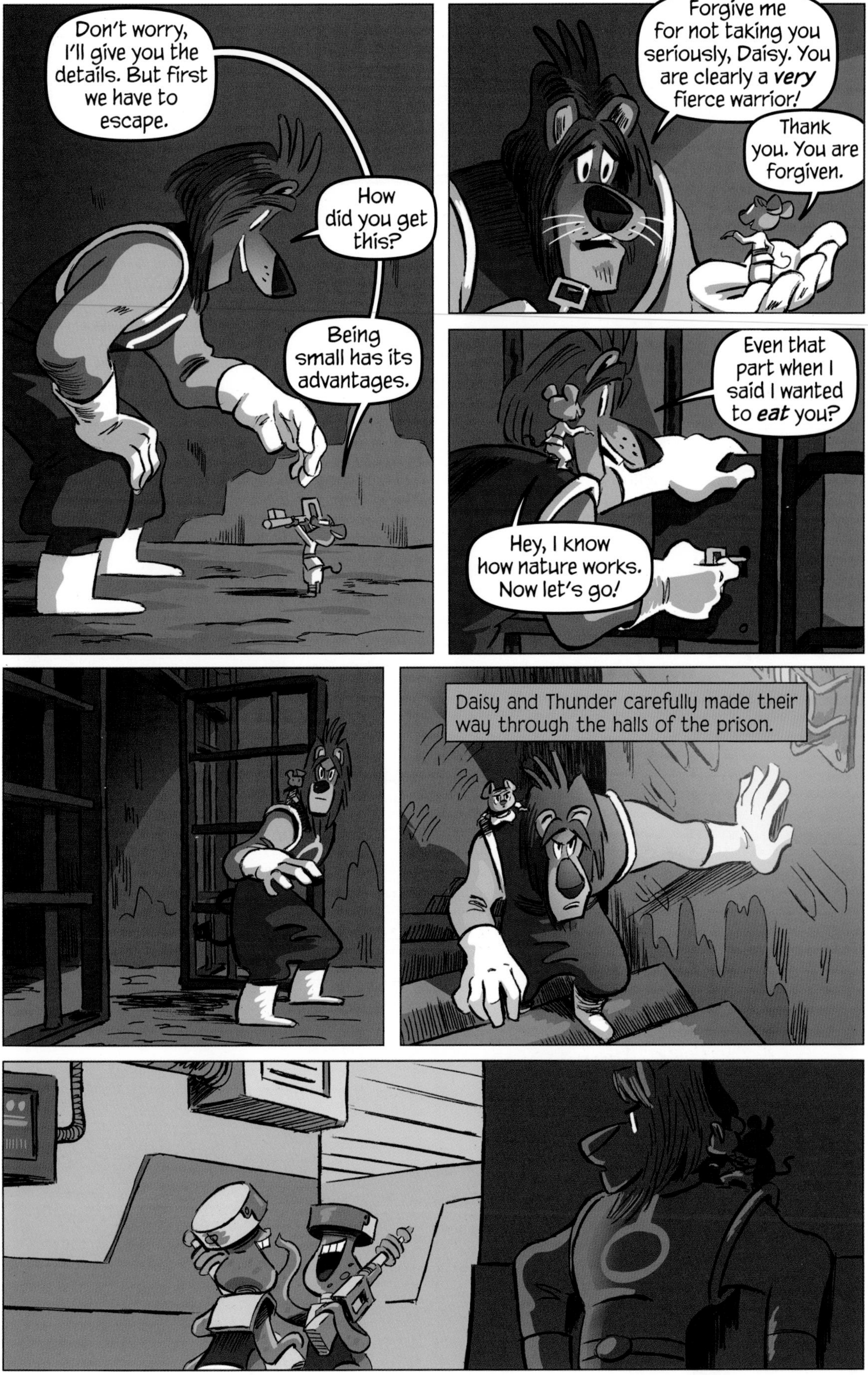
Don't worry, I'll give you the details. But first we have to escape.
How did you get this?
Being small has its advantages.
Forgive me for not taking you seriously, Daisy. You are clearly a *very* fierce warrior!
Thank you. You are forgiven.
Even that part when I said I wanted to *eat* you?
Hey, I know how nature works. Now let's go!
Daisy and Thunder carefully made their way through the halls of the prison.

Then Daisy used her smarts (and her teeth) to open the gate.

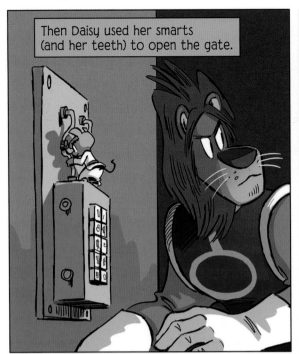

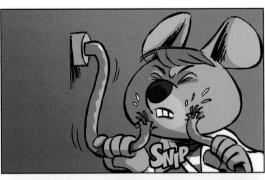

SNIP

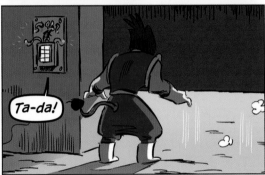

Ta-da!

We're free!

There's no time to celebrate. We have to get to the new Resistance base!

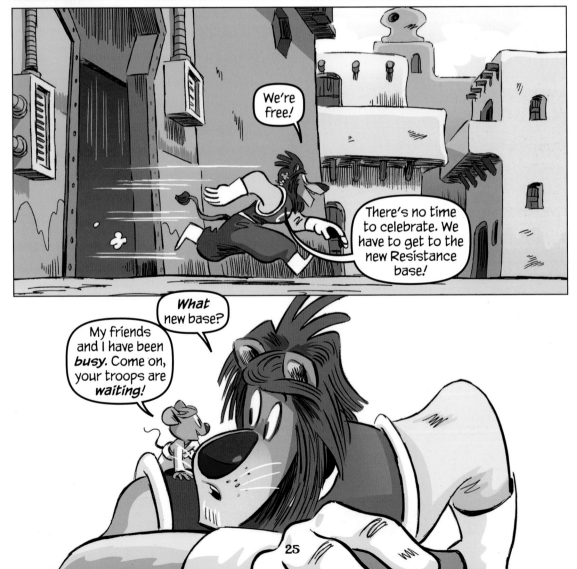

What new base?

My friends and I have been *busy.* Come on, your troops are *waiting!*

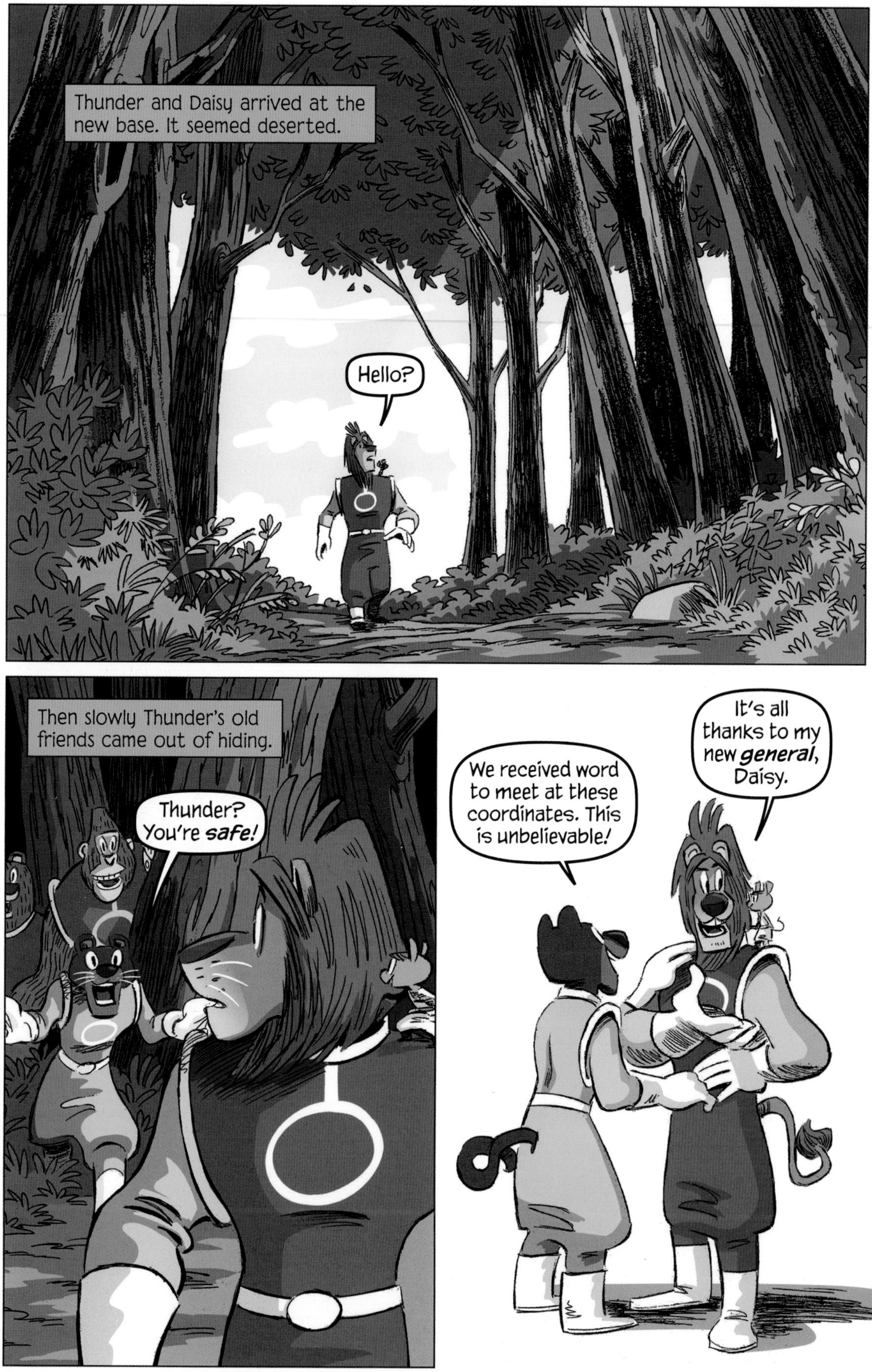
Thunder and Daisy arrived at the new base. It seemed deserted.
Hello?
Then slowly Thunder's old friends came out of hiding.
Thunder? You're *safe!*
We received word to meet at these coordinates. This is unbelievable!
It's all thanks to my new *general*, Daisy.

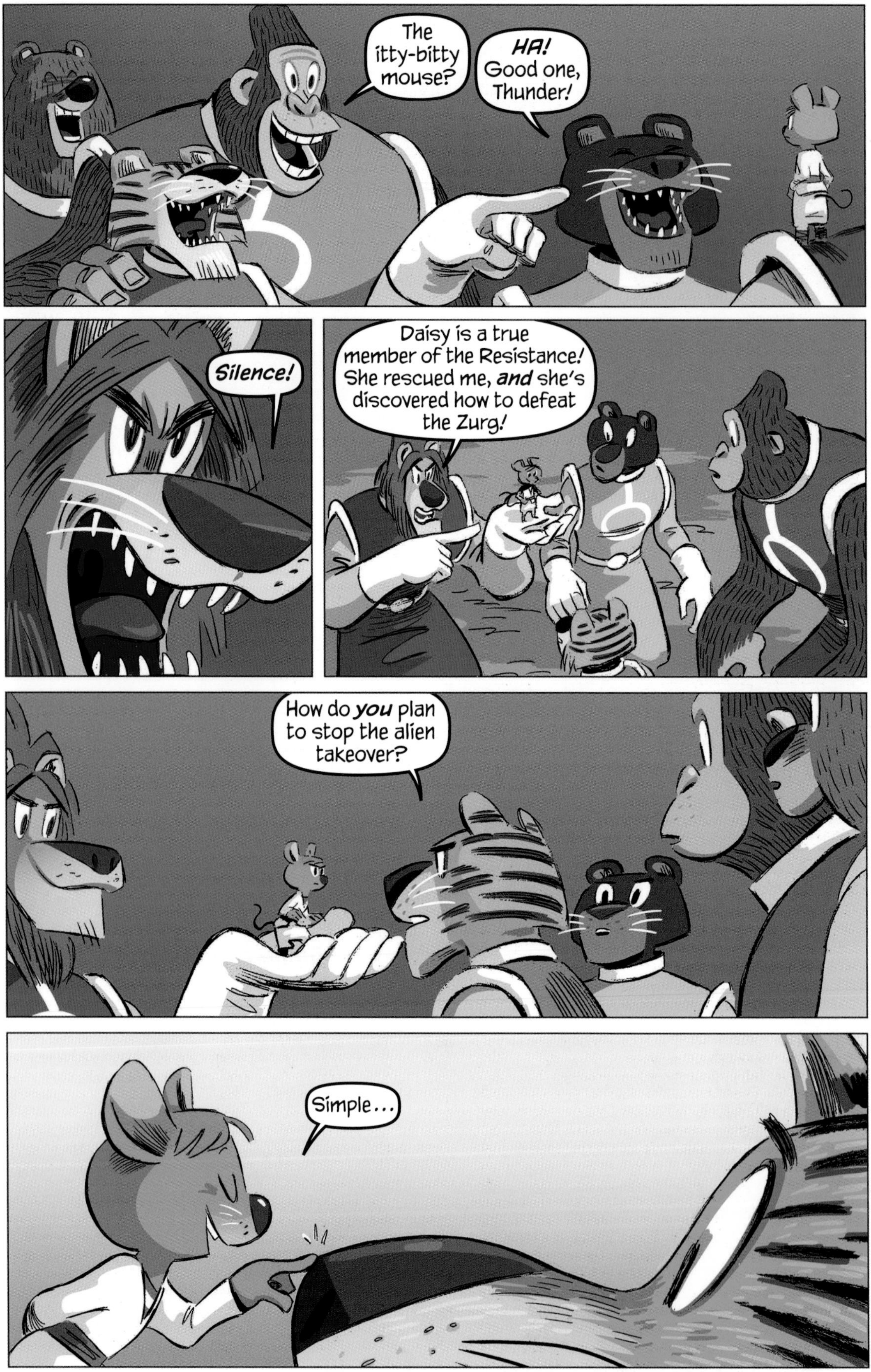
The itty-bitty mouse?
HA! Good one, Thunder!
Silence!
Daisy is a true member of the Resistance! She rescued me, and she's discovered how to defeat the Zurg!
How do you plan to stop the alien takeover?
Simple...

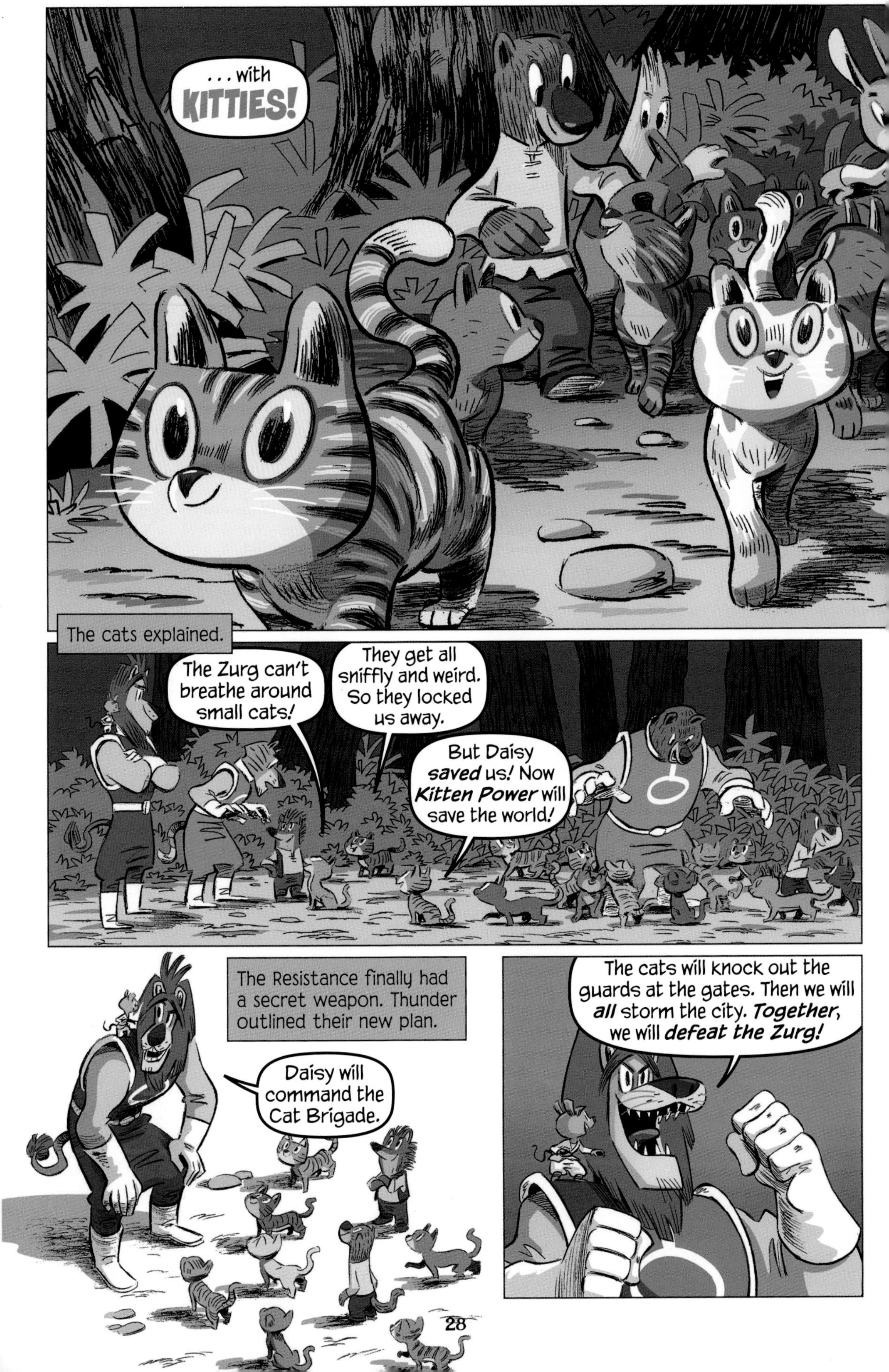

. . . with KITTIES!
The cats explained.
The Zurg can't breathe around small cats!
They get all sniffly and weird. So they locked us away.
But Daisy *saved* us! Now *Kitten Power* will save the world!
The Resistance finally had a secret weapon. Thunder outlined their new plan.
Daisy will command the Cat Brigade.
The cats will knock out the guards at the gates. Then we will *all* storm the city. *Together*, we will *defeat the Zurg!*

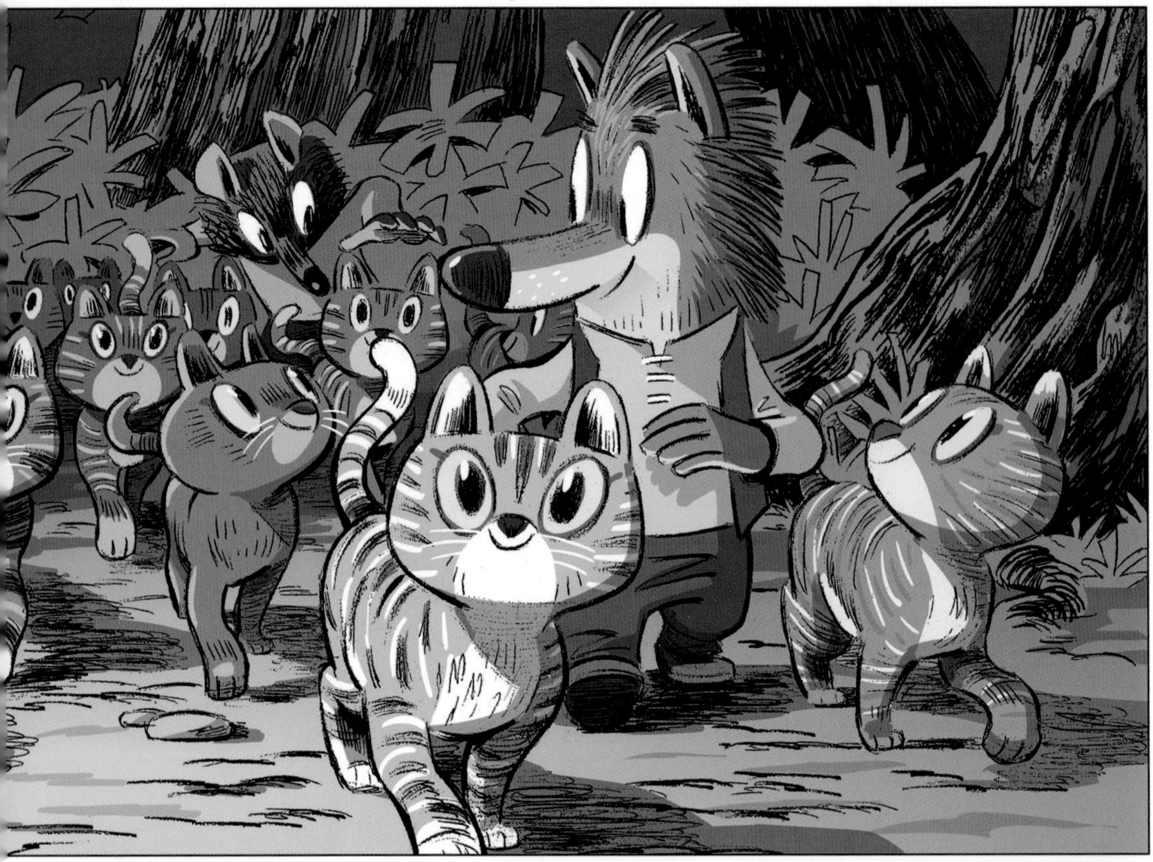

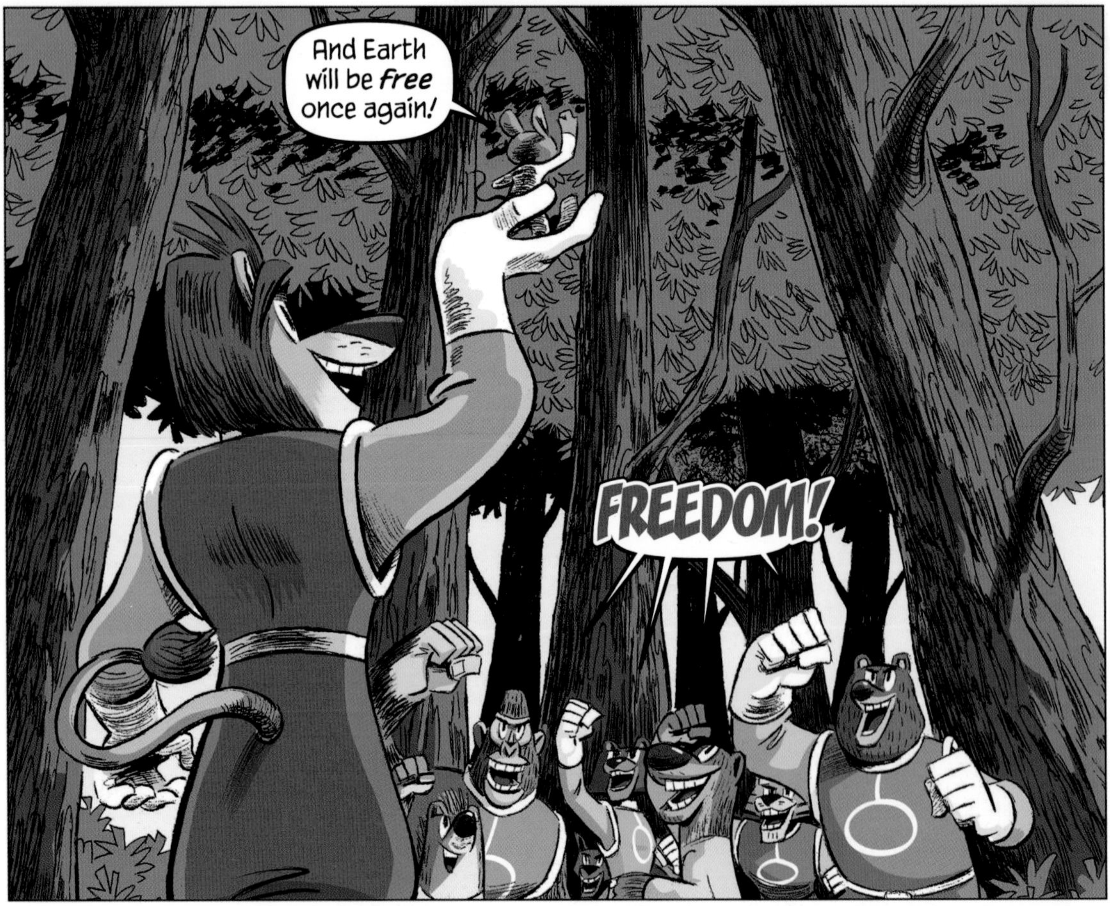
And Earth will be *free* once again!
FREEDOM!

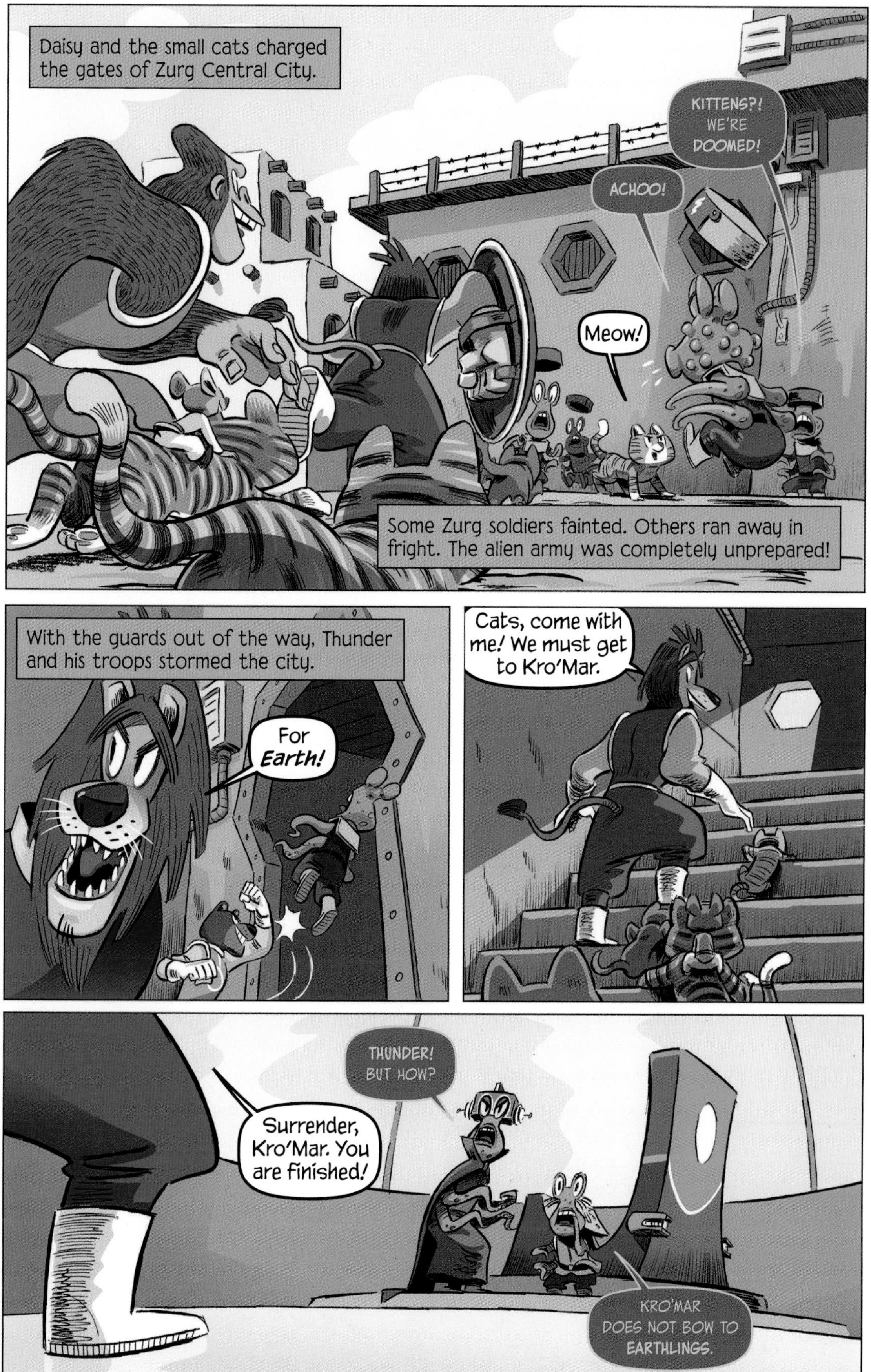
Daisy and the small cats charged the gates of Zurg Central City.
KITTENS?! WE'RE DOOMED!
ACHOO!
Meow!
Some Zurg soldiers fainted. Others ran away in fright. The alien army was completely unprepared!
With the guards out of the way, Thunder and his troops stormed the city.
For *Earth!*
Cats, come with me! We must get to Kro'Mar.
THUNDER! BUT HOW?
Surrender, Kro'Mar. You are finished!
KRO'MAR DOES NOT BOW TO EARTHLINGS.

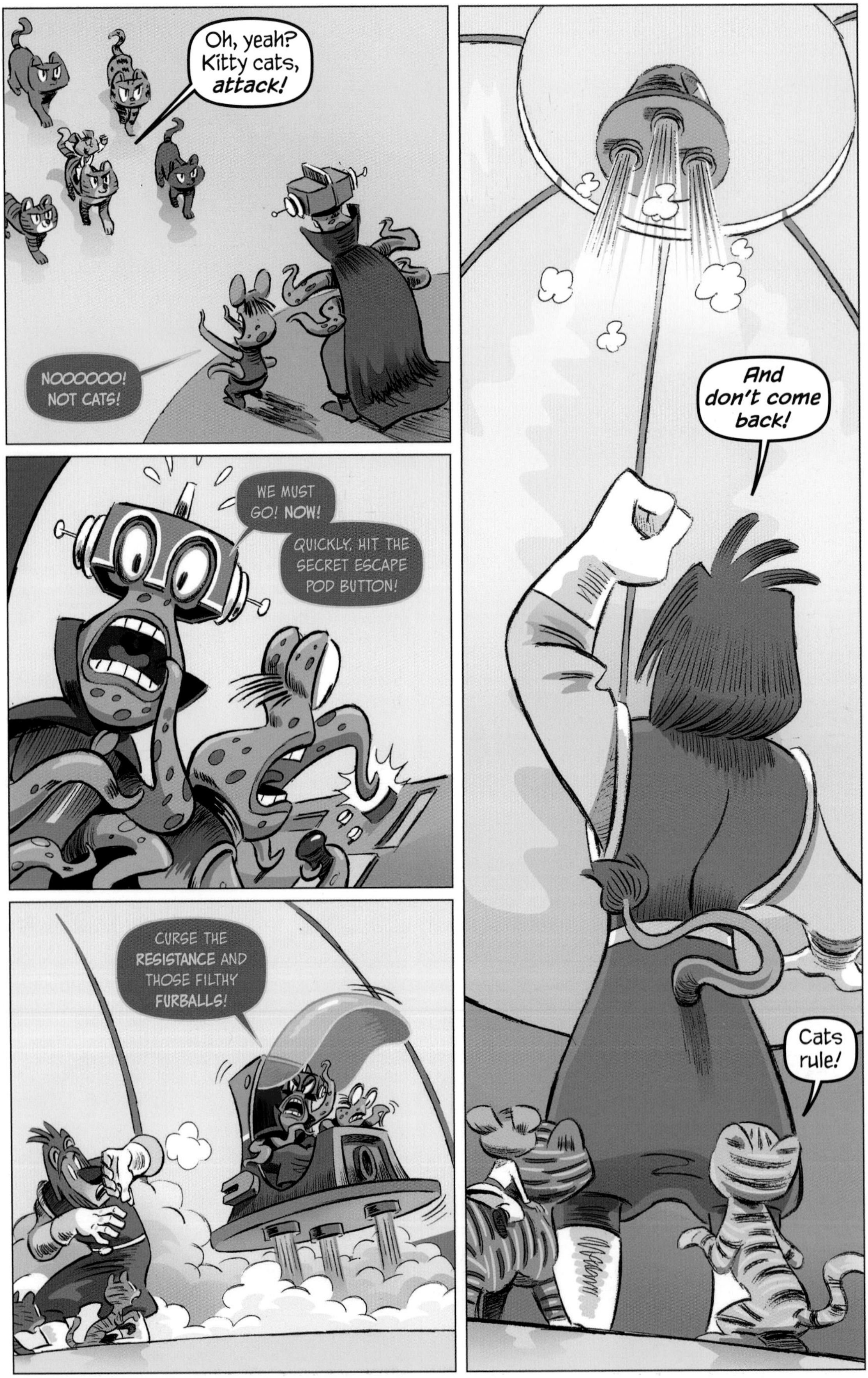

Oh, yeah? Kitty cats, *attack!*
NOOOOOO! NOT CATS!
WE MUST GO! **NOW!**
QUICKLY, HIT THE SECRET ESCAPE POD BUTTON!
CURSE THE **RESISTANCE** AND THOSE FILTHY **FURBALLS!**
And don't come back!
Cats rule!

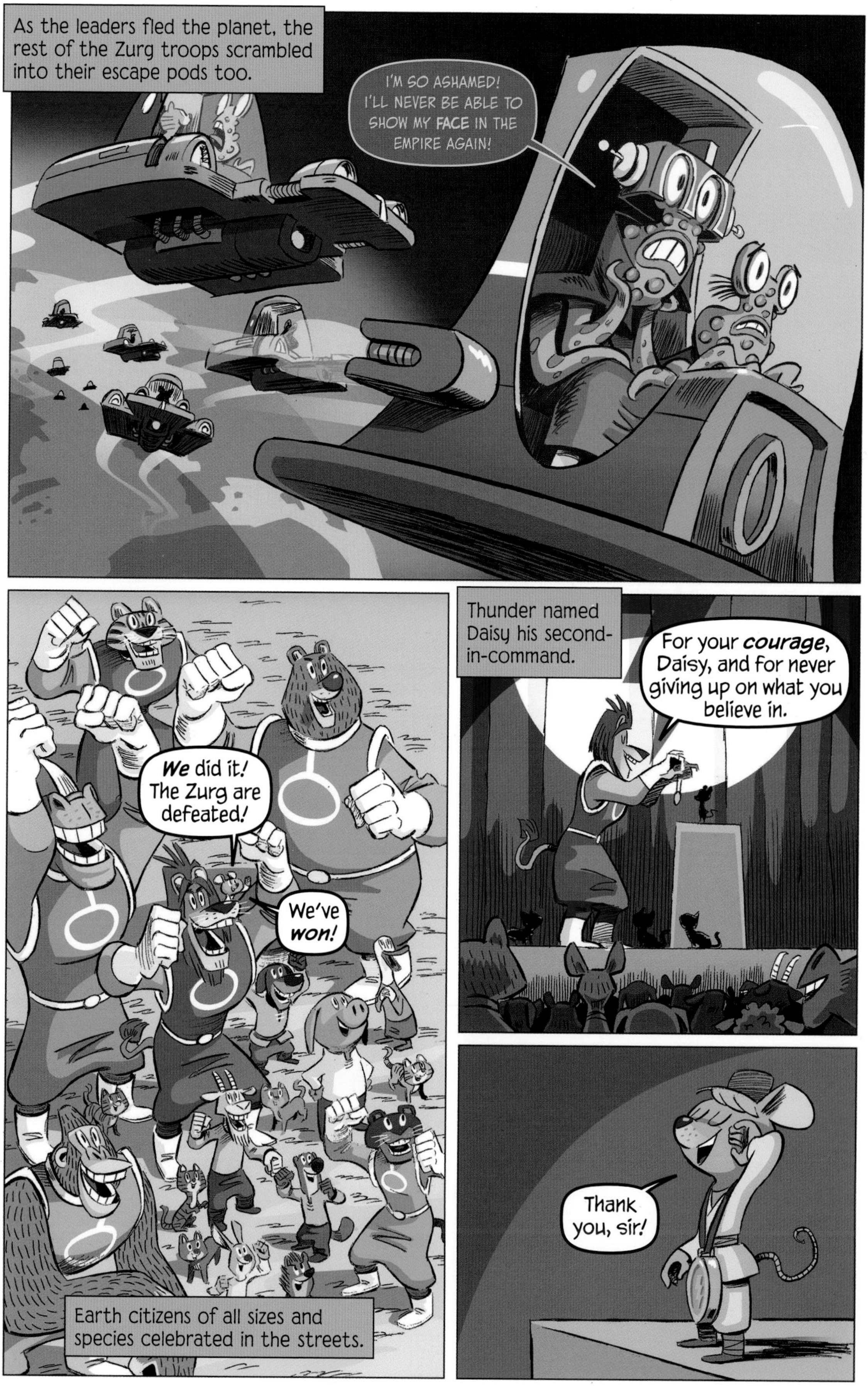
As the leaders fled the planet, the rest of the Zurg troops scrambled into their escape pods too.
I'M SO ASHAMED! I'LL NEVER BE ABLE TO SHOW MY FACE IN THE EMPIRE AGAIN!
We did it! The Zurg are defeated!
We've won!
Earth citizens of all sizes and species celebrated in the streets.
Thunder named Daisy his second-in-command.
For your courage, Daisy, and for never giving up on what you believe in.
Thank you, sir!

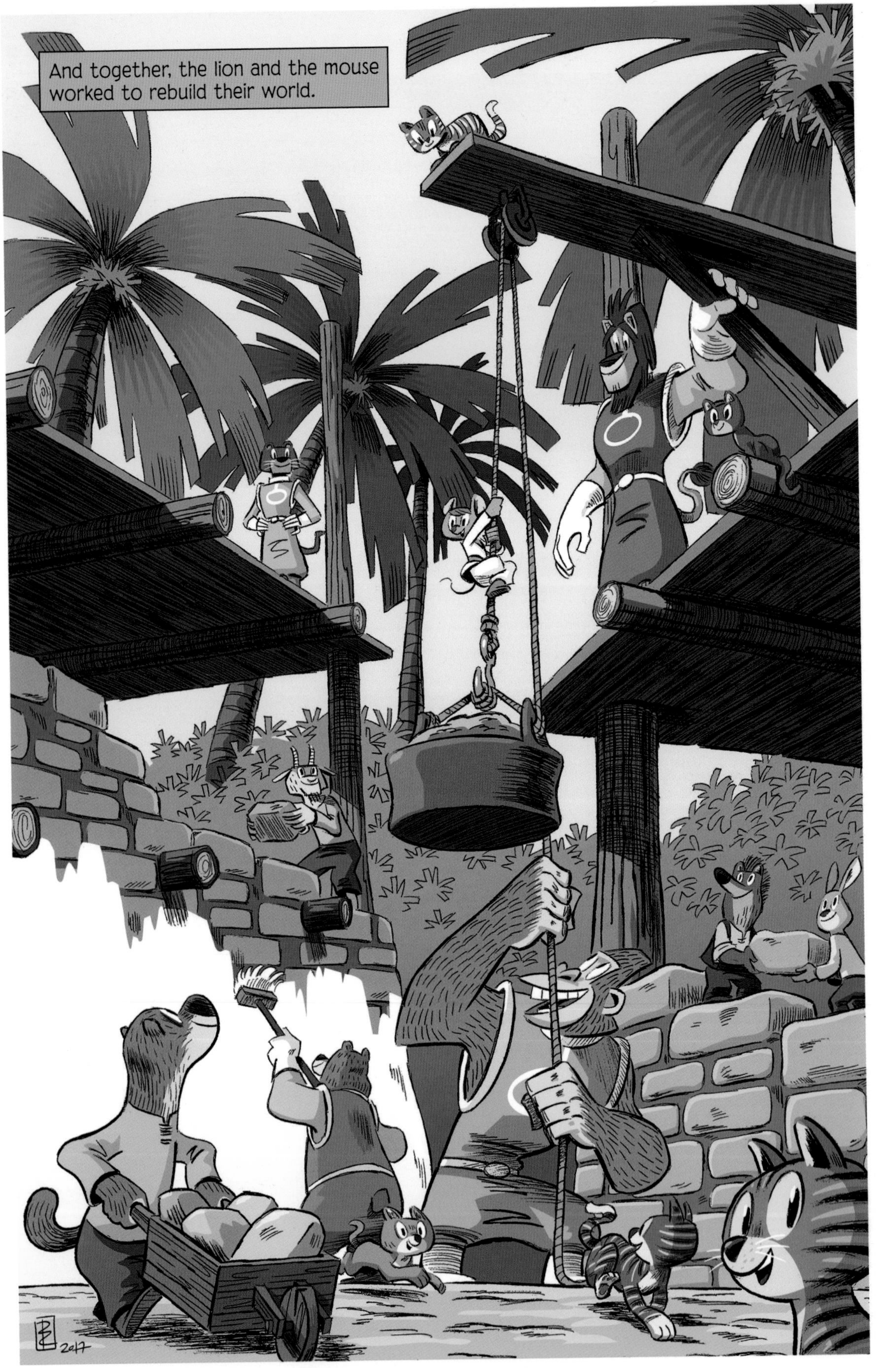
And together, the lion and the mouse worked to rebuild their world.

ALL ABOUT FABLES

A fable is a short tale that teaches the reader a lesson about life, often with animal characters. Most fables were first told thousands of years ago by a Greek storyteller named Aesop. At the end of a fable, there's almost always a moral (a fancy word for lesson) stated right out so you don't miss it. Yeah, fables can be kind of bossy, but they usually give pretty good advice. Read on to learn more about Aesop's original fable and its moral. Can you spot any other lessons?

THE LION AND THE MOUSE

One day, a mouse scurries across a sleeping lion. Lion wakes up and catches Mouse under his paw. He's about to eat the small creature. But Mouse cries out, "Please, mighty Lion, have mercy and let me go! In return, I promise to help when you are in trouble." Lion laughs. He doesn't think a tiny mouse would ever be able to help him, but he lets the rodent go. A few days later, a hunter's net snaps up around Lion. The big cat struggles but can't free himself. He roars in frustration. Mouse recognizes Lion's cries and rushes to the trapped animal's side. Mouse gnaws on the net. Soon he has chewed through the ropes and sets Lion free. "You laughed at the idea that I could help you," Mouse says. "But now you see that even a mouse can help a lion."

THE MORAL

LITTLE FRIENDS CAN MAKE GREAT FRIENDS
(In other words, don't judge people
based on their appearance —
looks don't matter
when it comes to
helping others!)

A FAR OUT GUIDE TO THE FABLE'S GALACTIC TWISTS!

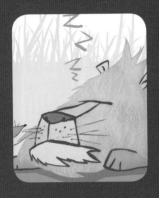

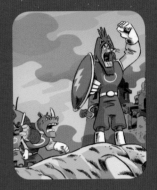

The lion in this version isn't napping – he's leading the Resistance and battling an alien army!

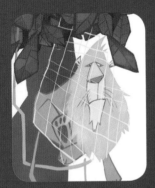

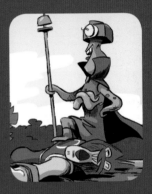

Lion is captured by hunters in the original. Here, Thunder is taken prisoner by Kro'Mar, the powerful Zurg leader.

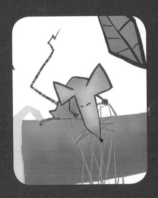

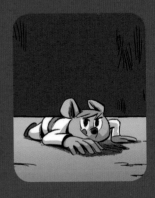

Daisy doesn't chew through a net. Instead, she bravely sneaks into a Zurg prison to rescue Thunder!

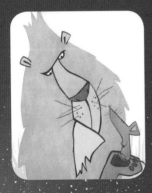

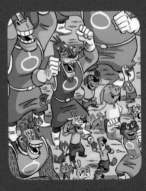

Lion and Mouse are the only animals in Aesop's fable. In this story, many big and small animals work together to beat the Zurg invaders.

VISUAL QUESTIONS

Describe what Thunder and his troops think of Daisy when they first meet. Use examples from the text and art to support your answer.

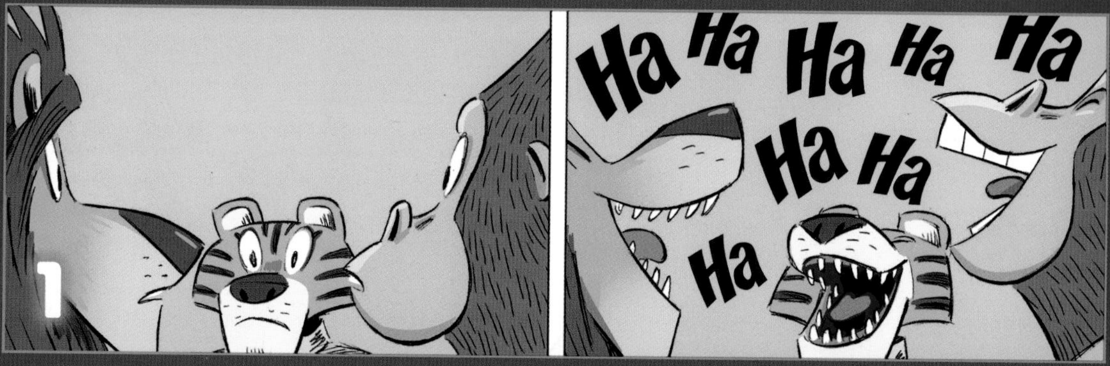
1
Ha Ha Ha Ha Ha
Ha Ha
Ha

The word "ZZZOOOONNG" is a sound effect, or SFX for short. They help show and describe sounds. Find other examples of SFX in this book. How are they used differently? Try designing your own SFX.

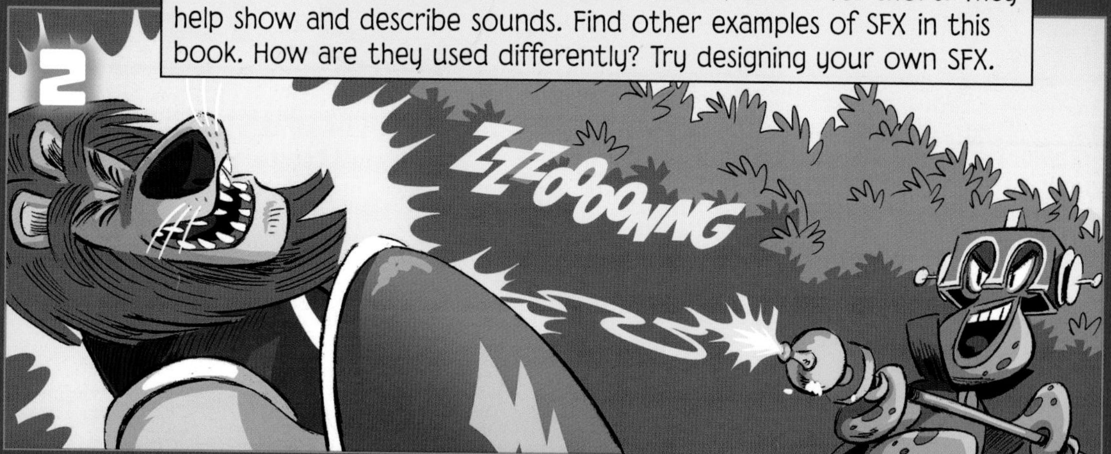
2
ZZZOOOONNG

In your own words, describe how the kitties helped the Resistance defeat the Zurg invaders.

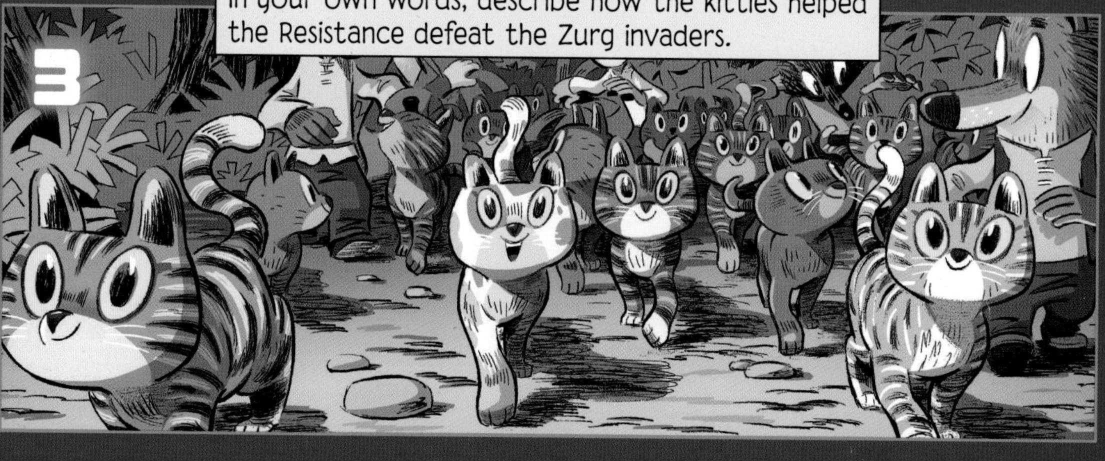
3

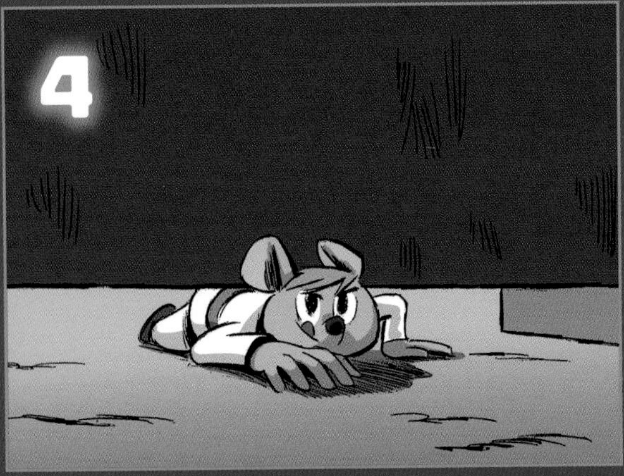
4

A theme from the original fable is that you shouldn't judge people based on their appearance. List three ways Daisy used her small size to fight the Zurg. Would Thunder or the other large animals have been able to do the things she did? Explain your answer.

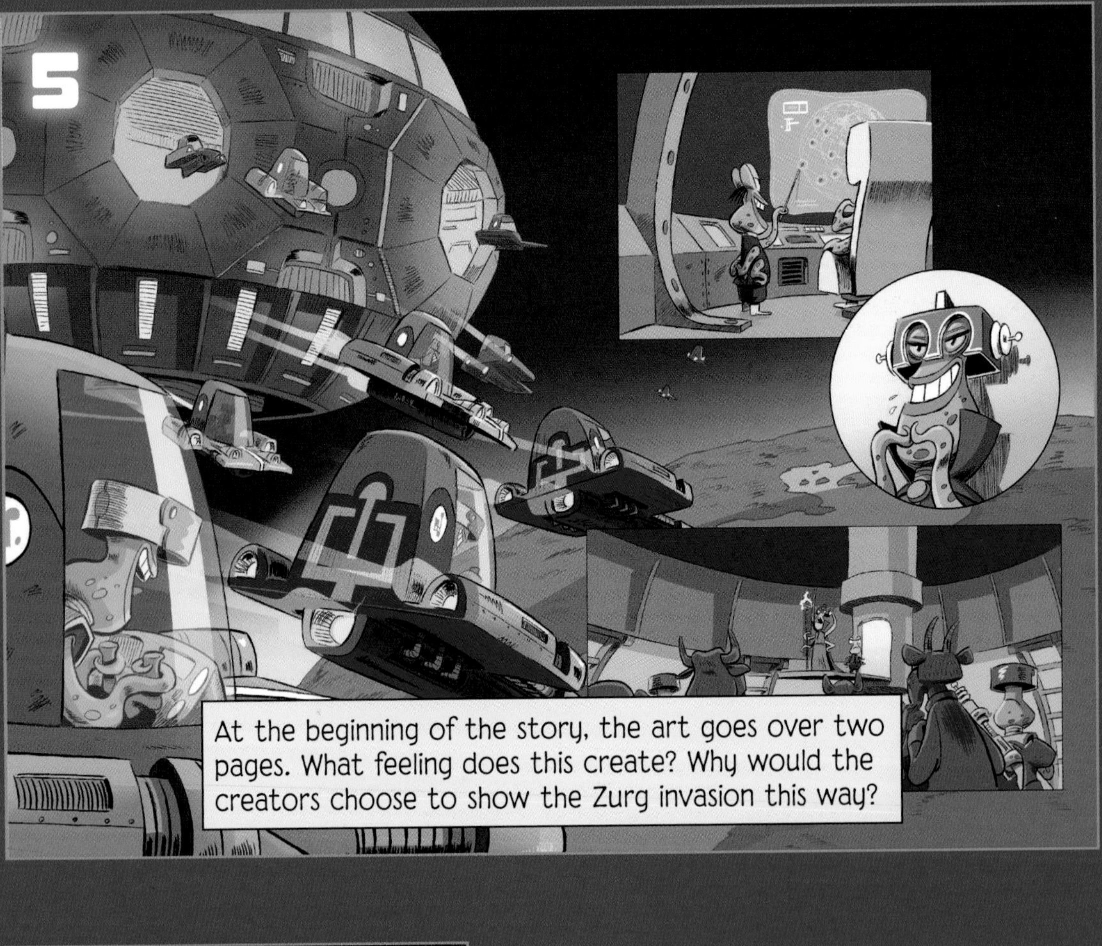
5

At the beginning of the story, the art goes over two pages. What feeling does this create? Why would the creators choose to show the Zurg invasion this way?

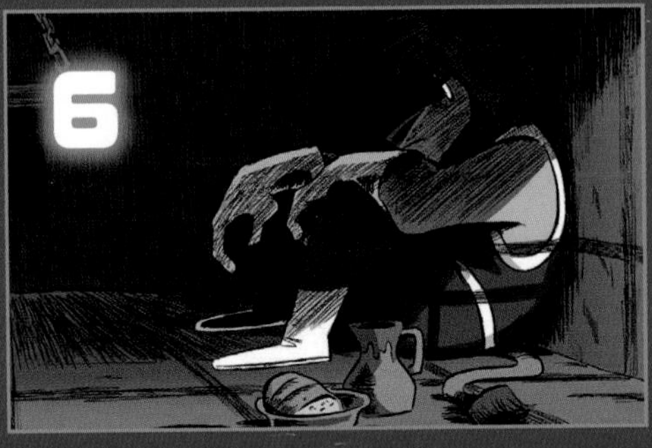
6

Even when characters aren't speaking, the art can give you clues about what they're thinking or feeling. How does Thunder feel here? What might he be thinking? Use examples from the art to support your answer.

AUTHOR

Benjamin Harper has worked as an editor at Lucasfilm LTD. and DC Comics. He currently lives in Los Angeles where he writes, watches monster movies, and hangs out with his cat Edith Bouvier Beale, III. His other books include *Obsessed With Star Wars*, *Thank You, Superman!*, and *Hansel & Gretel & Zombies*.

ILLUSTRATOR

Pedro Rodriguez studied illustration at the Fine Arts School in Barcelona, Spain. He has worked on a variety of projects in design, marketing, advertising, publishing, animated films, and music videos. He now has more than forty published books, including his award-winning comic book *Omar el Navegante* and a series of Rudyard Kipling graphic novel retellings he illustrated for Stone Arch Books. Pedro Lives next to the beach, close to Barcelona, with his wife, Gemma, and their daughter, Maya.

GLOSSARY

allergic (uh-LUR-jik)—having a harmful reaction to something; reactions often include sneezing, swelling, and rashes

ambush (AM-bush)—a surprise attack

conquer (KON-kur)—to defeat an enemy and take control with force

coordinates (koh-OR-duh-nits)—a set of numbers used to show the position of something on a map

debris (duh-BREE)—the pieces of something that has been broken or destroyed

invaders (in-VADE-uhrz)—armed forces that go into an area (like Earth!) to take control of it

malevolent (muh-LEV-uh-lunt)—having bad or evil goals; wanting to cause harm

meek (MEEK)—fearful and cowardly; if someone is meek, they obey others and don't argue

rally (RAL-ee)—to bring together and get ready for action

resistance (ri-ZISS-tuhnss)—a secret group that fights against an enemy that has taken control of the area

retreat (ri-TREET)—to move back troops on the battlefield because the enemy's attack is too strong

underground (UHN-dur-grownd)—done in secret and without approval from authorities

THE MORAL OF THE STORY IS... EPIC!

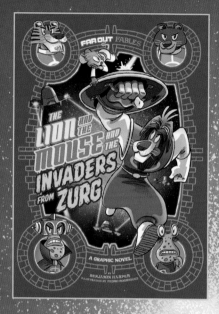

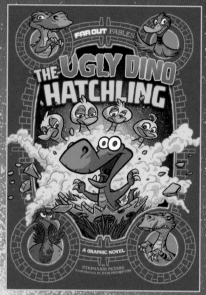

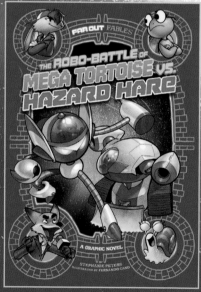

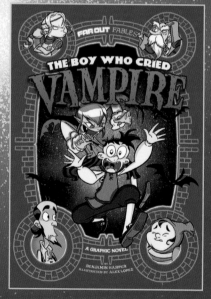

FAR OUT FABLES

ONLY FROM capstone

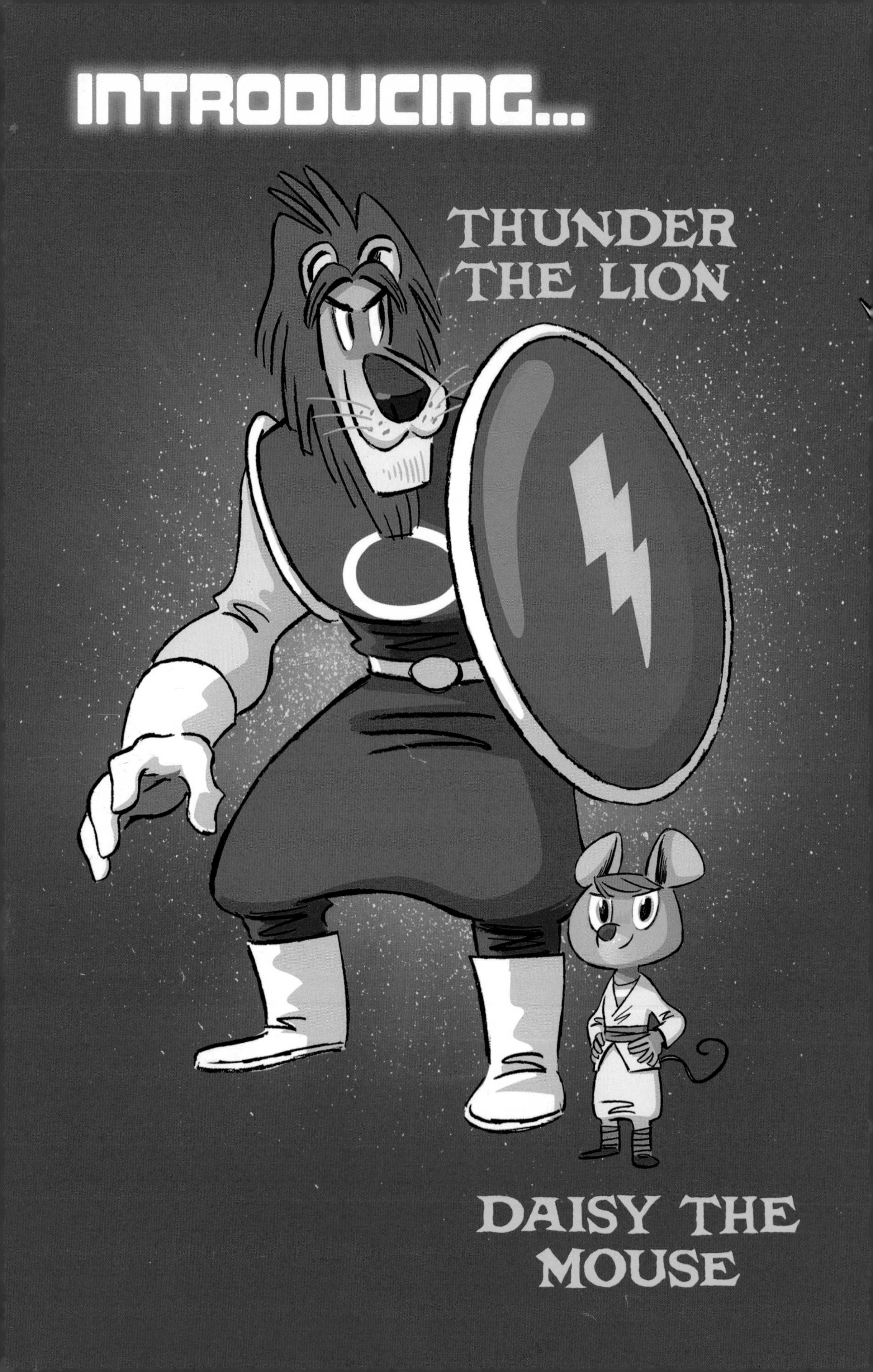
INTRODUCING...
THUNDER THE LION
DAISY THE MOUSE

FAR OUT
FABLES

STONE ARCH BOOKS
a capstone imprint